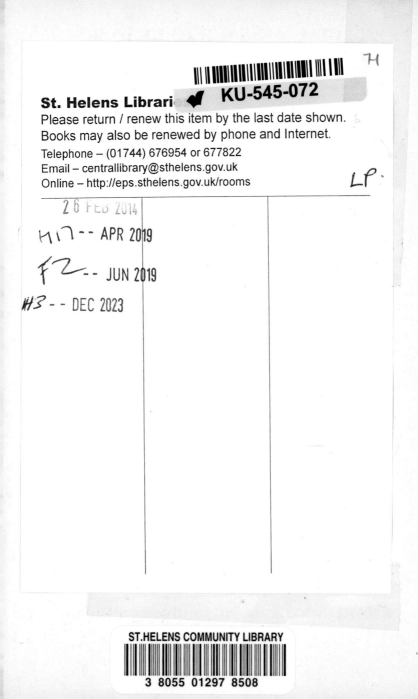

7H

St. Helens Librari ✔ **KU-545-072**

Please return / renew this item by the last date shown.
Books may also be renewed by phone and Internet.

Telephone – (01744) 676954 or 677822
Email – centrallibrary@sthelens.gov.uk
Online – http://eps.sthelens.gov.uk/rooms

LP

26 FEB 2014

H17 -- APR 2019

F2 -- JUN 2019

#3 -- DEC 2023

ST.HELENS COMMUNITY LIBRARY

3 8055 01297 8508

SPECIAL MESSAGE TO READERS

THE ULVERSCROFT FOUNDATION
(registered UK charity number 264873)

was established in 1972 to provide funds for research, diagnosis and treatment of eye diseases. Examples of major projects funded by the Ulverscroft Foundation are:-

* The Children's Eye Unit at Moorfields Eye Hospital, London
* The Ulverscroft Children's Eye Unit at Great Ormond Street Hospital for Sick Children
* Funding research into eye diseases and treatment at the Department of Ophthalmology, University of Leicester
* The Ulverscroft Vision Research Group, Institute of Child Health
* Twin operating theatres at the Western Ophthalmic Hospital, London
* The Chair of Ophthalmology at the Royal Australian College of Ophthalmologists

You can help further the work of the Foundation by making a donation or leaving a legacy. Every contribution is gratefully received. If you would like to help support the Foundation or require further information, please contact:

THE ULVERSCROFT FOUNDATION
The Green, Bradgate Road, Anstey
Leicester LE7 7FU, England
Tel: (0116) 236 4325

website: www.foundation.ulverscroft.com

ACE OF BONES

When famed gunslinger Reno Valance rides out, the instructions are clear: collect his wife's relative and return home. But for the man who used to be known as Ace, it turns out not to be so simple: Uncle Gifford is dead — murdered! Soon a world of evil is unleashed, and Reno is forced to make a decision. He's dealt the devil's card for twenty years, and now he'll have to do it once more, taking up his Remington as the Ace of Bones . . .

Books by Clay Starmer
in the Linford Western Library:

THE HIRED ACE
HELL AND THE HIGH S

CLAY STARMER

ACE OF
BONES

Complete and Unabridged

ST. HELENS COMMUNITY LIBRARIES	
ACC. No.	
CLASS No.	

LINFORD
Leicester

First published in Great Britain in 2012 by
Robert Hale Limited
London

First Linford Edition
published 2014
by arrangement with
Robert Hale Limited
London

Copyright © 2012 by Clay Starmer
All rights reserved

*A catalogue record for this book is available
from the British Library.*

ISBN 978–1–4448–1853–6

Published by
F. A. Thorpe (Publishing)
Anstey, Leicestershire

Set by Words & Graphics Ltd.
Anstey, Leicestershire
Printed and bound in Great Britain by
T. J. International Ltd., Padstow, Cornwall

This book is printed on acid-free paper

1

'Oh, Jeez,' Stan Gorman howled as a stranger pushed through the batwings of the Deep Gulch Hotel. 'I can't take no more.' He jabbed a finger at the upturned tables and broken chairs. 'What'll it take for you people to stop?'

The stranger shook his head. A moment later, his spurs clanking on the floorboards, he crossed to the long counter. 'Mister,' he drawled. 'You've had trouble, it seems. You'll get none from me. I just want liquor after a long trail.'

Stan studied this rugged newcomer with his dust-dressed clothes, two hundred pounds or more, Stan assessed, of pure sinew and muscle but the face spoke of age. Laying aside a broom then, the Deep Gulch's owner muttered, 'So you ain't with the Brand O?'

'No way,' responded the famed gunslinger Reno Valance, removing his Stetson. 'I've just touched town and I've a heck of distance to swallow.' Reno nodded at the back shelf with its slug-blasted bottles. 'Can you salvage a whiskey out of that?'

Stan's tenseness eased. 'I'll get you a beer first.' He stepped behind the counter and produced a flagon. 'If you've spent time in the saddle you've got to wash down the dust.'

Soon, with that flagon to hand, Reno fixed Stan with a questioning look. 'Brand O? I take it they're cattle men?'

Stan sighed. 'Well, yeah but . . . I mean . . . not really.' The hotel owner grabbed up a cloth and whipped it against the back shelf. 'Jeez,' he yelled, 'it ain't ropers or punchers what's done this.' He pinned Reno with an agonized stare. 'It's thug guns Sherman Lomax has took on lately.'

Reno pondered that a moment but then turned to his drink. He swallowed most of it, removing the flagon from his lips with a grateful groan before saying drily, 'I'd say your sheriff's got it tough about now?'

2

Stan's eyes widened. 'Sheriff?' he spluttered. 'I like the man but Hell — ' He broke off with a shake of his head before adding dejectedly, 'Wendell Polk gets to trouble in his own time and that's slow; thugs are gone before he gets here.'

Reno gave a laconic grin. 'He's afraid, eh?'

Stan returned a disquieted look. 'No, he's just too old.' The portly barkeep turned and lifted one of the few intact bottles. In no time, a glass filled, he passed a shot of whiskey over the counter. 'Here, salvaged like you asked for and on the house; there'll be no more of my woes. What about you?'

Reno shook his head. 'Like I said, I'm just after — ' He choked off as guns bellowed in the street outside.

Stan shook his head and, reaching down, hauled up a sawn-off. 'I've got the perfect remedy for those bastards.'

Reno was confused. The Gulch's damage suggested a hotel man not ready to wield a gun; that Gorman did

3

so now seemed odd.

'Are you set to use that?'

'It's not loaded,' Stan intoned. 'I've held off with it till now. It might make them think twice.'

Reno gave out a guttural growl. After a five-day ride, with 160 miles underfoot and his body and mind aching, he just wanted a quiet drink. What he didn't need was rowdy cattlemen and a barkeep brandishing an empty shotgun. Easing the Remington out of its low-cut holster, he moved toward the batwings.

'I take it,' parodied Stan as Reno closed on the swing doors, 'you're set to use *that*?'

'Yeah,' Reno answered testily, 'if I have to.' He paused then, listening intently as more gunshots roared in the street. When they'd faded, he heard a woman's pitiful wails. 'Goddamn it,' Reno spat. 'I'll make — '

A crash of the batwings stilled Reno's words and sent him fast to ground. Once down, perched on one knee with the Remington levelled, he tracked the stumbling entry of a man.

He didn't shoot, though. Through his gunslinger years, the ability to gauge others had served him well. Right now, he sensed the person entering the saloon proffered no threat. Aged about twenty or so, the kid wore a Colt at his right leg but his hands stayed shy of it. His sweat-plastered hair and wide startled eyes suggested he'd been the target of those shots outside.

Reno's judgement proved right. Soon, staring balefully at Reno's gun, the kid's face paled before he tore across the saloon and ducked down behind a piano.

Reno set to rise but a creak at the swing doors stilled him. He jerked his gaze about and tracked the entry of two men. This pair — all dusters and wide brims — held by the entrance with Colts in their hands.

'Stay down, mister,' one growled, eyeing Reno dismissively. 'This is Brand O business.'

The other scowled. 'The kid goes home; you stay out of it.'

The one who'd spoken first — a big-bellied man of middle age and at least a week's stubble — ran his gaze about the saloon.

'Where you hid, Terry? We're taking you to your pa to be beat.'

'Get to hell, Wilkes,' the kid's tremulous response came. 'He's not my pa and you know it.'

'He dragged you up,' growled the fat one. 'That makes him your pa in my book.'

When the kid suddenly showed, lurching up with his gun to hand, Reno acted fast. With his gunslinger speed, he dragged round the Remington and sent a slug that whipped the distance and clattered the Colt out of the kid's grasp. A moment after, with the six-gun's bellowing echo quieted, the fat man shook his head.

'Hell, mister,' he drawled, 'that was good shooting. Our boss Mr Lomax will be grateful to you.'

Reno shook his head. Who these people were or why they fought, he didn't care. They'd take this face-up outside.

'I stopped the kid blasting you,' he said fixing Wilkes with a non-negotiable stare, 'but in this saloon you'll leave him be.'

Wilkes's look darkened. He drilled Reno with rage-widened eyes. 'You done a favour, drifter. Don't be getting it wrong now!'

Reno shrugged. 'You've got choices like all men. Right now, you've got but seconds to make yours.'

Hesitancy showed in Wilkes's eyes. This rugged stranger in the Deep Gulch had the touch of a hard man about him; that shot to disarm Terry meant he knew his way about his Remington. Still, no matter a man's pedigree, most of them died in the end. Caution, though, swayed the fat man's judgement.

'You've marked your card,' he growled at Reno. 'We see you again you'll get sorry on it.'

He spun with that, cursing loudly as

he booted out at the batwings. When those swing doors settled to stillness — a drumming of hoof beats on the street proof enough they'd left — Reno holstered his gun and returned to the counter.

The kid soon joined him. Whooping, Terry retrieved his gun and bounded down to the long bar.

'God dang,' he said staring at Reno appreciatively. 'That quelled them.' He grinned broadly. 'Thanks, I'll stop in town till Pa calms down.'

Reno recalled the conversation between the kid and the men.

'You said he weren't your pa?'

'My step-father,' said Terry bedding his gun. 'Sherman Lomax he's named; he's the biggest pig this side of anywhere.'

It didn't take long for Terry to bring Reno up to speed. Here, in Seward County, one man controlled all. Sherman Lomax possessed the sprawling Brand O beef empire and his word stood as law. Though he'd always been a difficult man, since the death of Terry's mother five months before, Sherman Lomax had become hate-filled and destructive to both himself and the land's folk thereabouts. Gradually, loyal ranch-hands had either left or begun to grumble and Sherman had hired on any ruffian who happened his way. He wanted fast guns to keep his men at heel. For his favoured few — the quick draws — they had carte blanche to derive their entertainment any way they chose.

Terry, fleeing the ranch, had set to Arrow Town when he'd ridden straight into Kyle Wilkes and Max Solomon. Terry had taken a rapid detour but Wilkes and Solomon had ridden in pursuit.

'You riled your pa,' said Reno laconically. 'He'll beat you for it.'

'I'll get a whipping but I'll not be owned like a stinking steer.' The kid shrugged. 'I'll bunk at the livery and set home tomorrow when Sherman's wrath's lessened some.'

Terry went to step out of the saloon

but suddenly halted. 'I'm Terry Lomax. You are . . . ?'

'Reno Valance, kid, nice to have met you.'

Terry left and Stan Gorman shelved the shotgun. He fixed Reno then with an intrigued look.

'Now, why *are* you in Arrow Town?'

Reno explained: a number of letters from his wife to her only living relation had elicited no response. Anna May's uncle Leyton Gifford had not attended Reno and Anna May's wedding; with the baptism of their child coming up, Anna May wanted action. Reno would collect her uncle.

'Old man Gifford?' The barkeep shrugged. 'We don't see him in town but when he stocks up.' Stan looked mystified. 'I never figured how he makes his money.'

'Anna May,' responded Reno. 'She says Leyton's place is up in the Green Coat Hills a few miles north of Arrow Town.'

'Sure is. He's up there alone.' Stan

frowned. 'You'll go to the hills now — I mean, now you've tasted the problems here?'

'No,' Reno shook his head. The whiskey he'd consumed began to work its magic. 'I've earned an overnight. I'd look for good company, good redeye and a soft bed for easy sleep.'

'Mr Valance,' Gorman said breezily. 'If thugs stay away you'll get all three at the Deep Gulch Hotel.'

2

'Hell,' grumbled William McClure wiping a sleeve over his sweat-drenched forehead, 'this damn heat.'

McClure, a muscular, rugged-faced man with huge death-soiled hands and a filthy scar on his left cheek lifted himself in the saddle and looked around. To all sides the earth spanned to a far-blue skyline. McClure thought of the grave, spat angrily and, lifting the brim of his hat, fixed an old man on a buckboard with a piercing look.

'Mister, where've I got to?'

'It's Seward County, friend.' The wagon man, with a gap-toothed grin, jabbed a bony thumb south. 'Next stop Arrow Town.'

'That place amount to much?'

The man shook his head. 'It's just beef and hills about here. Oh, there's one old sheriff.' At that, he drove his team of two forward and had gone some way before yelling, 'Sheriff Polk couldn't hit a barn door if he was stood by it.'

McClure glared at those hills he'd just vacated. There, under the oak and hickory trees, a comfortable enough shack had been somewhat spoiled. Weeks before in one of the rooms, a body had bloodied the wall and floor when McClure had pumped the occupant with slugs. He'd dragged the old man's body out and left it in the scrub for consumption by critters. In no time, it had become disarticulated bones. Now, the man's stores depleted and McClure certain the posse that had chased him out of Missouri was gone, he'd exited that highland to peruse this unknown country.

McClure mused on that man he'd killed. He'd been a bit prickly at first but eventually he'd agreed to brew a coffee. Soon, he'd divulged some information — the most important being that few people frequented those hills.

A big mistake, the psychopathic slayer had chuckled when he'd rifled the dead man's pockets.

McClure hauled his thoughts to now. He cursed, spat at the parched earth and then watched the buckboard trundle out of view. A moment later, his mind made up, he set his mount toward Arrow Town. It sounded perfect.

Two hours' steady riding brought him there. Thus, with dusk making shadows, McClure walked his horse down Arrow Town's now almost deserted Main Street. He glanced about; his attention was drawn by lights flickering on in the buildings, but then diverted by some sort of disturbance further along the street. There, where a livery building had both its doors flung open, a blond-haired youngster had his arms out to his sides in a pleading way.

Terry Lomax, in fact, was desperate.

'Ah, come on,' he implored the liveryman Ben Moses, 'you've just got to let me stay.'

'I can't do it, kid,' resisted Ben not

wanting to get involved in another family squabble. 'You know that.'

'Please,' Terry whined. 'It's getting dark and I'll be in the street if you don't.'

'Damn it, Terry,' growled Ben then. 'Get in the hayloft and I best hope your pa don't show up here looking for you.'

Terry grinned and dived into the barn.

McClure took it all in and only moved his gaze away when he heard the sound of footsteps on the boardwalk nearby. He turned to see an elderly man standing there, the oldster's suspicious look replaced by a wheezy call.

'Good evening to you, stranger.'

'Yeah, yeah,' said McClure testily. He nodded toward the livery. 'What in hell's all that about?'

'It's Terry Lomax,' said the old man with a cackling laugh, 'staying out the reach of his pa's whip hand.'

It didn't take McClure long to glean the minutia of Terry's domestic travails. With that learnt, he walked his horse on. Soon, McClure and his mustang filled the livery entrance.

Ben, set to give Terry a piece of his mind, stopped short.

He studied this thickset drifter with the filthy looking face scar and gave an involuntary shudder. A moment later, though, he'd girded his nerve.

'I take it, sir,' proffered the livery-man, 'that you're looking to stable?'

'No,' growled McClure, 'I'm not stopping.'

Terry, seated on a hay bale, gave a nonchalant shrug. 'You've a good ride to the next town.'

'I'm not going to any next town,' snarled McClure. 'I'm here to take you home.'

Terry's face paled. An instant later, with his eyes widening and his lips starting to part, he inched to his feet and began to move toward the hayloft ladder.

McClure acted fast. He hurtled across the barn and pinioned Terry against the wall. In a blur then,

16

McClure clenched his fingers to a fist that he delivered viciously to Terry's jaw. The young man groaned, his knees giving way as he dropped senseless to the straw-carpeted floor.

Ben Moses shrugged. He'd seen Terry taken home so many times but they'd never beat him out cold before. He studied McClure and couldn't help but shudder again. The man's thickset frame and sinister eyes hinted at trouble; that scar on his face hinted at worse. Who in hell he was Ben could not fathom. Probably some drifter thug Sherman Lomax had recently taken on.

'Hey, feller,' said Ben dismissing his disquiet and patting a still-saddled quarter horse. 'You'll take this too?'

McClure nodded. He dragged up the stunned Terry and slung the young man face down across the saddle. Soon, lashing the kid in place, he led the horse and captured youngster through the doors.

He turned to glare at Ben. 'What way to Lomax's place?'

Ben's face clouded. 'Set west about

twelve miles and that'll bring you to Brand O land. The ranch-hands will see you coming right enough and take you to the big house.'

McClure mounted his own mustang with a satisfied grunt. A moment later, leading Terry's horse by the reins, he trotted off along Main Street. Closing on Arrow Town's western edge, McClure raked spurs and he and Terry disappeared in a maelstrom of dust.

Ben stood on the street awhile then he headed back into the livery. *Jeez*, he mused as he stepped into the forge. What he'd just witnessed made no sense at all.

*   *   *

Whilst Stan Gorman arranged for the stabling of Reno's pinto, his wife Mary boiled water for a bath. Later, Reno soaked in a tub. Immersed in the hot fluid, he listened to the noise of Main Street through the partly opened window of his rented room.

He heard shouts and drumming hoof-beats of horses as they galloped along Main Street but he couldn't rouse himself out of the delicious enfold of soapy suds to look out.

He thought of Anna May and longed for her. A few days and he'd hold her once more. He felt good as the water soothed his hurting body. He ached not only from the rigours of the long ride, but for his wife and son. Tomorrow, Leyton Gifford in tow, he'd set home to White Falls.

* * *

McClure sat impassively in the saddle as two Brand O men drove their mounts towards him.

When they got there — the last dulled light seeping off the land now — they stared aghast at Terry roped to his saddle.

'Hell,' muttered Wilkes staring inquisitively at this rugged trespasser. 'You've brought Terry from town?'

19

McClure smirked. 'Yeah,' he drawled. 'I reckoned Mr Lomax might be glad to have the kid brought home.'

Solomon nodded. 'I reckon so. Thanks, we'll take him in.'

McClure shook his head. 'I got to speak with Mr Lomax.'

'Can't do it,' growled Wilkes. 'Mr Lomax don't like drifters.' He jabbed a finger at McClure's face. 'How'd you manage that scar?'

McClure spat at the earth and then said icily, 'I don't see Lomax then you don't get the kid.'

The Brand O men levelled their carbines.

McClure, drawing a knife from his belt, angled his mount around Terry's horse to a point where he could grip the youngster's hair and drag his head up. This done — Terry emitting a distressed grunt — McClure applied the knife's gleaming blade to the blond-haired youngster's throat.

'No,' Wilkes bellowed frantically then, 'not that.' He lowered his gun and nodded at Solomon. Facing McClure again, he growled, 'OK. We'll ride you in.'

They kicked their mounts on, McClure still leading Terry's horse, and in less than an hour, they'd crossed the now night-swamped grassland to where a barrage of illuminated windows announced the Brand O homestead. As they got closer, McClure gave a whistle of admiration. It was an impressive spread — the Palladian house set at one side of a quadrangle of stabling and utility buildings. Enough men filled the area, some smoking outside huts whilst two stood guard at a gate as they rode in.

Dismounting by a corral, Wilkes pointed to the ranch house.

'I'll go and tell Mr Lomax.'

'No need, Kyle. I'm here.'

They turned to see Lomax step out of one of the huts. He perused McClure before settling on the tethered form of his son.

'This feller picked him up, Mr Lomax,' drawled Wilkes. 'He said he had a need to speak with you.'

Sherman fixed McClure with a stern look. 'That right?'

'Yeah,' returned McClure drily. 'We need to talk.'

Sherman nodded. 'Wilkes, lodge the kid in the barn. I'll beat him later.' He nodded at McClure. 'You come with me.'

As McClure followed Sherman toward the big house, Terry's cries filled the yard.

'You sons of bitches,' the youngster howled as Wilkes and Solomon loosed his binds and then dragged him to the barn.

He shouted on a while, but no one was listening. With Wilkes and Solomon in the long-hut set aside for the hired guns, McClure sipped brandy with Sherman Lomax in his office.

'The boy's a worry,' drawled Sherman. 'He won't see sense.'

'So I heard,' said McClure. 'That's why I brought him.'

Sherman nodded. A moment later, out of his seat, he strode to a safe set low down into the room's rear wall. He crouched, deftly spun the lock and drew open the stronghold's door.

McClure, turning in his seat, craned his neck to get a sight of the safe's contents. Dollars were in there, stashed high. Sherman immediately slammed the door shut and crossed to a shelf. He reached into a vase and withdrew some money. In no time, he'd slapped five twenty dollar notes on the desktop.

'That's payment for your deed.'

'It's a shame,' said McClure pocketing the greenbacks, 'that I can't offer you something in return.'

Sherman frowned. 'What are you saying, mister?'

'You need a gun and a man good behind it?'

'Those men Wilkes and Solomon,' said Sherman with a shrug, 'they're quick-draws out of Montana. I took on others too.'

McClure began to build a smoke. 'I don't know the names. I'm in the gun game and if they were top drawer I'd have heard.'

'And you?' drawled Sherman. 'You're top drawer?'

'There's none better,' retorted McClure. 'You got troubles I'll tend to them.' He completed the cigarette, lit it, and blew out a perfect circle of grey smoke. He anchored the ranch boss with a piercing look. 'Like I say, I'm the best.'

'Right,' said Sherman with harsh eyes. 'You're taken on. I got need for skilled gunmen and I'll reward you well enough.'

McClure nodded. 'OK, Mr Lomax. I won't let you down.'

Sherman waved a hand in dismissal.

'Get to the bunkhouse and settle in. I'll tell you when you're needed.'

McClure rose to leave when Lomax spoke again.

'Say, what's you name, anyhow?'

'William V. McClure,' the scar-face said with a wink, 'out of Missouri.' Then the outlaw left.

McClure crossed the lamp-lit yard and whistled as he moved. Here, at the Brand O, he'd have his biggest payday.

3

The next morning broke hot over Arrow Town. Reno woke early, got his gear together and then enjoyed a breakfast served by a chatty Mary Gorman. Afterwards, he bid his farewells and set out to collect his horse. He'd only progressed a few yards along the boardwalk when he found his way blocked by an elderly man with a star pinned to his chest.

The ageing lawman perused Reno up and down before muttering, 'I heard a stranger hit town yesterday.'

Reno shrugged. 'Today that stranger's leaving.'

'Green Coat Hills,' said the lawman. 'I heard that's where you're set.'

'Is there a problem?' growled Reno studying the sheriff's aged features and deciding he couldn't be less than sixty.

'I'm Wendell Polk,' the sheriff muttered. 'I've been law in this town nigh on thirty years and most of it good. Right about now, you'll be minded, things have got a bit different.'

'Listen,' retorted Reno with impatience showing in his voice. 'I'm here to bring my wife's uncle to a baptism. I'm sorry for your problems but I leave as soon as my pinto's saddled.'

Sheriff Polk gave a protracted sigh. 'Too many leave Arrow Town — good folk gone on account of this trouble. This town's dying. He shrugged. 'I can't keep these hoodlums in check.'

Reno couldn't stop himself barking testily, 'I already — ' He left the rest unsaid and perused the sheet of crumpled paper the sheriff had taken out of a pocket and thrust forward. Reno read it before returning it to the lawman. He'd seen it before.

'You're he,' said the sheriff. 'You're the quick-draw they call Hired Ace.'

'I was,' said Reno more gently now. 'I'm deputy sheriff of White Falls; I already said why I'm here.'

'Yeah,' said Polk turning away. 'Give

26

my regards to Leyton. It's a while since he stocked up.'

The sheriff shuffled away along the boardwalk and Reno strode on. He'd paid the hotel bill and before long — the livery fee settled with the assistant as Ben Moses was tending a breached mare — he set out of town.

In no time, in the saddle and at the town's western edge, he raked spurs. Arrow Town lay behind him now.

★   ★   ★

Terry, left roped up in the barn overnight without food or water, took his beating the best way he could. The pain was unbearable; the fact that those scum guns Wilkes and Solomon and that new scar-faced thug were all there to witness it made it even worse. Time after time, his step-father applied the birch cane but Terry bit down his cries. He took it in silence.

'You disobedient pig,' his father raged a dozen strokes into the punishment.

'You start to behave else you'll suffer.'

When it ended, with Terry's shirt shredded and his flesh lacerated and dressed with blood, Kyle Wilkes and Max Solomon walked away.

Only McClure stayed. He cut the young man down and lay him face forward on the barn floor. He worked off Terry's shirt and began to wash and dress the wounds.

'I don't get it,' winced Terry when he'd revived enough to sit up. 'You knock me out, drag me here to be beat and then help me.' He shook his head. 'Hell, I just can't work it out.'

'You don't know much, kid,' said McClure with a smirk. 'I got to get your pa's trust.'

'He's not my goddamn pa,' spat Terry. 'My pa — '

'Yeah, yeah,' interrupted McClure. 'I heard about that.' He squatted next to Terry and said in a hushed tone, 'You hate that man what beat you?'

Terry's eyes blazed. 'I hate the man right enough.'

McClure nodded. 'He's rich, this step-pa of yours?'

'He's got more dollars than you'll ever see,' growled Terry with contempt. 'I keep telling him to pay me out — twenty thousand he'd not miss and it would set me up handsome.' He eyed McClure suspiciously before grumbling, 'Who the hell are you, anyway?'

The outlaw smirked. 'Bill McClure's the name, right out of Missouri.' He fell silent a moment before saying tersely, 'That safe he's got would take some filling.'

'What're you saying?' answered Terry nervously.

'If I killed Sherman,' McClure went on, 'you'd be the ranch boss, right?'

Terry's look darkened. 'Listen, I don't like the way this talk's going. I might hate my pa but I wouldn't wish him or any other man dead. No, all I want is twenty thousand lousy dollars to leave for good.' Terry shook his head. 'I don't want to run the Brand O. The truth is I can't stand beeves.'

McClure shrugged. 'So it's just greenbacks for you?'

'Yeah,' Terry drawled. 'It's just twenty stinking thousand dollars.' His face contorted with bitterness. 'He won't give me the money and he won't let me leave.'

McClure moved over to the barn doors and gazed out at the yard. A while after, facing Terry again he said in a hushed tone, 'There could be a different way.'

Terry's eyes showed his confusion. 'Go on, then.'

'I've done kidnapping before.'

'Kidnapping?' Terry gasped. 'What the — '

'You said yourself,' cut in McClure, 'that your pa would be about desperate to keep you hereabouts. If he knows I got you and might kill you to boot, what d'you reckon he'll pay?'

'What it took,' said Terry. 'Mind, he'd gun you down first.'

'Don't worry on that,' retorted McClure. 'I can stay alive. Think, kid, he pays forty thousand we can split it.

I'll get a payday and you'll have enough to set up some place else.'

Despite his misgivings, Terry mused on the idea. The more he thought about it the more plausible it seemed.

'And Pa wouldn't get hurt?'

'Hell, no way,' said McClure with a grin. 'No one would. He leaves the money some place, we pick it up and split it and that's that. You'll have your twenty grand and I'll be gone.'

Terry nodded.

'Yeah,' returned McClure making his way to the barn's entrance again. Through one of the large ranch house windows he observed Sherman Lomax decanting a bottle.

Sup it up, McClure intoned as the cattle baron brought a glass to his lips, *you've not got many drinks left in this world*.

★ ★ ★

Reno gently lifted the skull and then lay it down again in the underbrush. There,

31

in the half-light and intense scented heat of the forested slope of the hills, he felt his guts lurch. He'd viewed and perpetrated violent, bloody acts all his life but the realization that the skull he had touched had been Leyton Gifford made him feel physically sick.

Cursing softly, Reno searched the shack. He found the killing room, spent slugs littering the floor and that crimson-stained wall. In a drawer in a sideboard, he located Anna May's opened letters. He pocketed them and checked on.

An hour later, with no clue to the killer found, Reno took a canvas sack and collected all of Leyton's bones. Finally, full of despondency, he led his horse down the slope towards the grassland. He'd return to Arrow Town.

Old Leyton — his beloved wife's only relation — was no more.

⋆　⋆　⋆

Evening approached when Sherman Lomax left his office and headed upstairs.

Wilkes and Solomon had hauled Terry into the house where the outfit's cook had bandaged the boy. Now, in his room and facedown on his bed to protect his wounds, Terry grunted as Sherman barged in through the door.

'You learnt your lesson, kid?'

'Get out,' spat Terry without moving.

'Aw,' Sherman retorted. 'Don't be sour with me. I only did it for your own good.'

Terry rose slowly to a seated position. His whole body hurt, but he anchored his stepfather with a scathing glare.

'It don't matter how often you beat on me, I won't be broke.'

'I got to,' implored Sherman. 'I got to get you ready to take on the Brand O. I got to make you strong to keep it.'

Terry shook his head. 'I'm not like you. I don't — '

Sherman sank to his knees and he began to sob.

'I miss your ma, Terry, every second of every day.'

'We both do,' Terry bellowed. 'But

33

hating the world because she's died isn't the way to do it.' He churned inside. He hated Sherman Lomax in a way that had no measure. Yet, right now, the cattle baron had played right into his hands. Terry got to his feet and stepped across to the brutal beeves tyrant. He knelt before the cattle magnate.

'You know I care about you, Pa,' he said softly, 'even though you hurt me like this.'

Sherman, tear-filled and repentant, threw out his arms.

'You're all I got, Terry. Don't leave me!'

'I want to stay, Pa,' Terry returned through gritted teeth. 'I'll do what you say. I'll be good from now.'

They embraced, Terry nestling his head on his stepfather's shoulder.

'I knew you'd stand by me and the brand,' drawled Sherman after a time. 'You're my son again.'

'Yeah, Pa,' returned Terry with his eyes blazing. 'Don't let anything break us up again. No matter what it costs you got to keep us together!'

4

With a lamp ignited against the gathering dark, Sheriff Polk took a coffee pot off the stove in the jailhouse and filled two tin mugs with steaming liquid. Passing one to Reno, they both slid into chairs either side of the law office's battered desk.

'I just can't take it in,' muttered Polk putting down his mug and fumbling for some makings, 'Old Leyton dead?'

Reno sipped at the strong coffee and shook his head. 'Anna May will be shattered by this.'

With a sigh, Polk lit his built cigarette and blew out a cloud of sweet-smelling smoke.

'I don't know what to say, Valance. There's not a chance in Hades we'll find the killer.'

Reno nodded. 'I'd reckon not.' He empathized for his wife's grief but he muttered practically, 'I'd best stay about town a day or two. Leyton needs to be laid to earth.'

Polk sighed. 'We haven't got a preacher but I'll say a few words on a casket if you'd be OK with that?'

Reno finished his coffee and stood up. 'I'll let Stan know I'm staying.' He produced the letters from Anna May he'd recovered from Leyton's place. 'He got the mail but didn't reply.'

Polk shrugged. 'The pony express dropped those letters in to me; I got one of the men from town to deliver them.'

'So why didn't Leyton write?'

Polk shook his head. 'Whenever I saw Gifford in town I'd ask him if he was leaving any mail to be taken on. I didn't know who'd written to him, of course.'

Reno's look was grim. 'I just don't understand; he used to visit Anna May when she was younger.'

'That man turned sour as he aged,' said Polk. 'He got troublesome as the years went by.'

Reno frowned, trying to make sense

of it all. At length he muttered, 'I guess so.'

'Talking of trouble,' Polk went on. 'I heard thugs shot up the Gulch twice yesterday.' He couldn't disguise a look of shame. 'They were out of town before I could get to them.'

Reno frowned. 'You said yourself you're getting on.'

'Yeah,' growled Polk. 'At least they stayed clear of town last night.' The aged sheriff shrugged. 'Who knows when they'll ride in again?' Polk threw up his hands. 'It's best to warn you.'

Reno made for the door but halted.

'You should give that badge up,' he said. 'Retire.'

'People need me,' said Polk sombrely. 'I can't do much, Valance, but I'm all they've got . . . '

★　★　★

Sherman Lomax, light-headed but not quite drunk, staggered out of the ranch house door and navigated his way to bunkhouse Number 1. Reaching it, the ranch boss steadied himself against the doorframe, belched loudly then tried to settle his sight against the scene inside. With night set across the quadrant now and the hut illuminated only by a solitary kerosene lamp, it took the cattle baron a few moments to get everything in focus.

This hut, set aside for the ranch guards and the hired guns, was sparsely populated. Two of the guards — Cain and Phillips — stood station at the gallows gate entrance as they did daily. Others had set out for the spread's boundaries for night hawking duties. Only the self-professed quick-draws were in the sleeping quarters. Kyle Wilkes, Max Solomon and McClure all sat on the ends of their respective bunks smoking.

'Listen,' drawled Sherman. 'I've settled my strife with Terry. It's a thing to be drunk on.' He thrust out a hand full of dollar bills. 'Ride to town and enjoy yourselves.'

Solomon smirked and took the proffered money. 'Hey, thanks, boss.'

Sherman stumbled away and Wilkes laughed loudly.

'Hell,' he enthused. 'I'll drink some.'

The fat-bellied Montana man kicked out at the leg of McClure's bed. He'd barely withdrawn his foot before McClure rose fast and clamped his hands about Wilkes's throat.

'Do that again, pig gut,' spat McClure pressing at Wilkes's jugular, 'I'll rip out your goddamn neck.'

Wilkes's eyes flickered with terror. A second later, he wheezed, 'Sure thing, feller.'

McClure loosed his grip and as Wilkes sank to his knees, gasping for air, the rugged Missouri outlaw spat at the floor.

'I'm set for sleep. I've trailed some miles.'

Wilkes, regaining his composure, threw a venomous look at the scar-faced Missouri man. A second later, he'd gotten to his feet and stalked out through the hut door.

'Say, McClure,' drawled Solomon

before leaving. 'Don't mind, Kyle. You sure you don't want in on this money?'

McClure shrugged. 'That's what I said.'

Solomon shook his head. 'OK, we'll set to town. Your time will come.'

Soon, with the noise of drumming hoof-beats fading, McClure eased on to his bed and slid his hat over his face.

'Yeah,' he whispered. 'My time will come right enough!'

★ ★ ★

The tallboy clock against the saloon wall struck 11 p.m. and as a man played piano tunes to a handful of clientele, Reno abandoned any pretence to sleep and headed to the bar.

Stan Gorman greeted him with an understanding nod.

'Polk told me about Leyton. Why didn't you mention it when you booked in again?'

Reno shrugged and took the shot glass of whiskey the barkeep proffered.

'I'm not sure, Stan. It's shook me for sure!'

'Listen,' said Stan sonorously. 'If you need money to bury — '

'It's OK,' Reno cut in. 'I've got the funds for that.' He shaped to say more, but a rumbling explosion of thunder stilled his words. As that booming sky-roar petered out, rain lashed at the saloon's windows.

Stan beamed. 'Oh, thank the Lord.'

Soon, the mother of storms erupted onto Arrow Town. Lightning flashed its shuddering ferocity through the Deep Gulch's windows; more thunderclaps crashed over the settlement's roofs. Before long, a deluge of rain hammered at clapboard and glass with a drumming intensity that stilled the saloon's clientele of talk.

As the drinkers in the saloon listened with wordless awe to the weather's cacophonous noise, two men drove their horses up Main Street.

At a hitching rail close to the Deep Gulch Hotel, they stilled their mounts and eased out of the saddle. Soon, their horses tethered, they set to ascend to the boardwalk.

Across the street, peering out of the jailhouse window, Sheriff Polk gave a soft curse before drawing the curtains closed. A second later, he grabbed his Spencer Carbine off the desk. With the weapon loaded, Polk dragged on a coat, snuffed out the office lamp and then stepped on to the rapidly dampening boardwalk. Above him, rain cascaded off the walkway's awnings, splashing on to the town's central thoroughfare where it pooled fast and turned the street to a quagmire.

Despite the ferocious squalls and his failing eyesight, Polk quickly identified who'd just ridden in.

Kyle Wilkes was there, his ample proportions unmistakable; Max Solomon's profile was also easily recognizable.

'Damn Sherman Lomax,' muttered Polk. 'You take on such thugs.' Still, as he'd told that feller Reno Valance, he'd been sheriff nigh on three decades and

42

he'd honour his badge through good times and bad. Those thugs had shot up Arrow Town twice the day before and Polk let it go. He would not let it go right now.

The aged sheriff pondered on Valance again and his mood changed. Yes, one Reno Valance: a professional gunman, albeit one that sat behind a law badge now. He'd be in the main bar of the Deep Gulch at that very moment and the close proximity of a skilled killer gave Polk heart. He'd confront Wilkes and Solomon and warn them against future disorder in town.

Polk resolved to act decisively and fast. The two Brand O men, their horses lashed, had ascended the steps to the saloon's batwings.

The sheriff hurried into the street, his footfalls splashing in pools and his head bent against ceaseless, squalling rain.

'You men,' he bellowed. 'Just wait there.'

Despite the drumming intensity of the storm and the pounding of the piano keys drifting out through the Deep Gulch's swing doors, Polk's words reached the two Brand O men. Wilkes and Solomon stopped, turned in unison and then matched steps on to the sodden thoroughfare.

'You talking to us, old timer?' drawled Wilkes.

Polk gripped the carbine in both hands and shook his head.

'I'm old,' he spat, 'but it means I've seen a heck of trouble. Right now, I'll make sure no trouble bothers this town.'

Max Solomon shrugged. 'Go sit in your rocking chair then I reckon it won't.'

Sheriff Polk shook his head. 'It won't if you two saddle up and ride on out.'

'God dang,' said Wilkes loudly, 'We're aching for liquor and you expect us to forget it! There's no chance, Grandpa.'

'I'm saying you'll leave,' said Polk, nervousness turning his stomach. He'd hoped the noise of the confrontation would have drawn people out of the saloon but no one showed. Rain slammed on to walls and windows, the piano tunes just kept coming. Between them, they ensured no one in the hotel would hear anything of this altercation in the street.

Wilkes pushed the confrontation further.

'Get lost, old man. We're getting drunk.'

Wilkes went to turn but Polk jabbed at the overweight man's side with the muzzle of the carbine.

'Someone's in the saloon who won't let you cause trouble.'

'Is that a fact?' growled Wilkes inching his right hand toward the butt of his strapped-on Colt. 'That man got a name?'

'Reno Valance,' barked Polk. 'He's a hired gun and from what I've heard he's the best there is.' Polk felt sick to his stomach. He'd set Valance up but that might be the only way to get these Brand O hoodlums to go.

'That'll be him,' snapped Max Solomon. 'That'll be the hard case what stuck in with young Terry yesterday.'

'So he's still here,' snarled Wilkes. He hauled out his gun. 'We'll not give way to Mr high-and-mighty Reno Valance again.'

'You sure about that, Kyle?' responded Solomon anxiously. 'I mean, if he is a quick-draw?'

'Get some guts,' spat Wilkes. 'There are two of us.'

They ascended then, re-climbing the steps to the boardwalk whilst Polk was left to steel his nerve. He did it, levelling his carbine and glowering after them with a renewed rage.

'One foot more and so help me — ' Polk's words faltered. Cursing inside, he dropped the carbine and lurched forward. Belying his age, the sheriff reached Wilkes before the big man had his boots on the boardwalk. Polk clutched at Wilkes's arm and spat angrily, 'I said — '

His order ended as abruptly as his

life did. Wilkes, despite his size, spun fast. His gun barked in his grip, a sheet of flame flashing out as a slug ripped into Polk's guts sending the sheriff crashing into the muddy street. There Polk stayed — his hat knocked off and the rain thinning the blood that leaked from the wound to his stomach.

Reno, at the bar in the saloon, reacted fast. He could pick out a gun blast in any bedlam of noise. He had his Remington to hand and was soon booting open the batwings. All he saw on that rain-lashed road was Arrow Town's sheriff of thirty years lying dead, and a couple of horses charging at full pelt into the distance.

5

Men from the saloon carried the corpse of the sheriff across to the jailhouse and Reno arranged it on one of the cell bunks. Afterwards, he found a small crowd in the law office.

Stan Gorman sank on to one of the chairs; he looked bereft.

'Poor old Wendell,' he said morosely, 'What do we do now?'

Reno shrugged. 'Those riders what high-tailed it away — any of you men mind who they might be?'

The group of locals exchanged glances and then, one by one, they all shook their heads.

'None but you saw them,' protested Stan, 'how can we say?'

Another voice cut in then — a woman's voice.

'It'll be those thugs off the Brand O.' Mary Gorman stepped into the jail. She looked tense — a pinched set about her eyes and her face pale. She laid a hand to her rain-damped hair and then sighed. 'It'll be them — all here know it.'

'God alive, woman,' Stan exclaimed turning in his chair. 'It's one thing Brand O hoodlums busting up the Gulch; it's a whole bit different laying the murder of a sheriff at their feet.'

'It'll be them,' continued Mary, unfazed. She folded her arms and fixed Reno with a piercing look. 'Polk's wife and child died years ago. It's a wrong relief that none's left to mourn the man.'

Reno shrugged. 'Death's got too many ways.'

'Yeah,' said Mary curtly. 'We know all about death. When our parents built this settlement, Apache and rough guns killed so many they called Arrow Town the place of bones.' She shook her head. 'We've had peace since, but now . . . well; you've seen how it's got.'

Reno nodded as Mary spun about

and stalked to the door. She halted then, unfolding her arms and thrusting a hand into the pocket of her apron. A second later, she jabbed out with a handful of dollars.

Reno shook his head. Even though he suspected the answer, he still asked drily, 'What's that for?'

'Bounty, Mr Valance.' She glared at the huddle of locals. 'Are there men enough to ride with you as a posse?' She tossed the dollar bills on to the floor and plunged out into the rain.

The silence that settled after her departure lasted for some time. Finally, Stan Gorman broke it with a soft curse.

'My wife's taken on,' he muttered. 'She'd no place to do it.'

'No,' growled another. 'Mary's right — I'll ride.' The man who'd spoken — tall and attired in a suit — nodded at Reno. 'My pa rode on a posse and it's time I did too.'

'Richard,' drawled Stan. 'Are you sure on this?'

'Yeah,' the bespectacled man said.

50

'I'm Callaghan, Mr Valance, and I've got the hardware.' He ran his gaze about the others in the jail. 'Fellers, you'll ride with me?'

Soon, although most looked ashen-faced at the prospect, a few men nodded assent.

'Trouble is,' said Callaghan pleadingly. 'What's the point of a posse without a man skilled to lead it?' He shook his head. 'When all's said and done, Valance, we are only store keepers.'

Reno sank on to the chair behind the law desk and slid off his Stetson. He studied the locals with worry gnawing at his guts.

'Listen,' he intoned. 'There's nothing to be done tonight. I figure those Brand O men won't touch town again for a while. Be at the Deep Gulch midday tomorrow. We'll sort something then.'

The men filed out of the jail. Stan held by the door.

'Valance,' he intoned. 'Maybe Brand O killed Leyton as well?'

Reno gave a curt nod. 'Yeah — I aim

51

to find that out.'

Stan shrugged. 'Like the wife said, we'll pay what you want.'

Goddamn it, Reno muttered to himself after the hotel's owner had exited. He'd just become the Ace of Bones.

★ ★ ★

The Brand O complex was silent as they rode in. A few night-hawkers at the spread's eastern edge acknowledged their return, but as they let their mounts pick their own pace through the now unguarded gallows gate, it seemed all slept.

They dismounted and led their horses over to the stabling.

'Jeez, we've got to get away,' spat Solomon. 'We could have a rawhide end on this night's work.' Solomon shook his head. 'Hell, Kyle, why'd you blast that old sheriff anyhow?'

'He pushed too far,' spat Wilkes. 'You've killed enough!'

'Sure,' drawled Solomon. 'But I never shot a law; I never killed in a main street where we could've been seen.'

'No one saw,' Wilkes growled. 'That street was empty.'

Ten minutes later, their horses unsaddled and placed in stalls, Wilkes and Solomon set toward the bunkhouse.

McClure, illuminated by a kerosene lamp hung on the door post, drew on a smoke and blocked the way.

'You're awake?' said Solomon edgily. 'I thought you felt busted from the trail?'

McClure shrugged. 'I couldn't sleep; it's how it goes.'

Solomon nodded before adding grimly, 'Yeah, I reckon as I'll struggle for sleep myself.'

Wilkes lanced his partner with a scathing look.

McClure tossed aside his smoke and nodded. 'What sits in a man's mind he shares with few — maybe them he trusts . . . sometimes.'

Wilkes took a deep breath and made his own mind up. He still seethed over the set-to with McClure in the bunk-house earlier, but he resolved to bring the Missouri man up to speed. He wasn't sure why. Maybe, he mused, it was better to have this scar-faced brute on their side than against them.

'Listen,' Wilkes said. 'You can trust us.' He jabbed a finger toward the stables. 'But trust runs both ways.'

Soon, inside the barn where horses kicked against their stall boards, McClure closed on the two Montana men.

'You're back early; you don't smell liquored up.'

Wilkes shook his head. Though hatred of McClure turned his guts, he growled. 'A stranger's in town and is useful with a gun.'

McClure's eyes narrowed. 'Go on . . . '

'This stranger,' Solomon added then, 'wears a Remington slung right. He's tough looking and *I* wouldn't reckon to test him.'

McClure shook his head. 'God alive, say it's not him?'

'That man,' growled Solomon, 'you know him?'

'Say he's a thickset bastard,' spat

McClure, 'and rides a pinto. Well, yeah, I'd know him then.'

Wilkes's eyes flashed with worry. 'His name's Valance.'

'Yeah,' spat McClure. The outlaw turned toward the doors. Now, with the rain easing and the clouds beginning to dissipate, he seemed to be appraising the silver completion of a luminous full moon. When he looked back, he wore a look of foreboding. 'He's a gunslinger. We've never met, thank hell. Still, he's the kind of man what comes after me.'

Wilkes shuddered. He'd taken the slain sheriff's words about Valance as bluff. Yeah — that thickset drifter could handle his gun but many men could in these violent times. Most killed when they needed to and left other slayers alone. Bounty men, though, a very different breed, pursued through hell and high water those that spilt blood with their guns.

Wilkes shook his head. 'We'd best get out of here.'

McClure chuckled. 'So we've all got

a price on our heads?' Silent then, his face contorted as he battled his thoughts. He weighed it all up and finally growled, 'He must've locked horns with that Missouri posse. They'd have set him this way.' McClure spat at the dirt. 'He can't have got a bead on me. Hell, I hid for weeks in those hills.'

'What're you saying?' muttered Wilkes discomforted.

McClure winked. 'We'll ride out of here but first there's some dollars to be got.'

Solomon shook his head. 'We can't rob in town?'

McClure smirked. 'I've done a deal with that kid Terry.'

'Terry?' Wilkes snorted. 'That fool no-good he's — '

'He's a man that hates his pa,' snarled McClure. 'He's also a kid that's worked it out.' He smiled then. 'I'd say you two can be trusted. Now, how'd you boys fancy being in on a good deal?'

Wilkes and Solomon exchanged furtive glances.

'Go on,' rasped Wilkes, 'we're listening.'

At that, McClure told them. As he drawled off — a short silence enduring through which each man considered the risks and gains — Wilkes grinned.

'Goddamn it,' he muttered, 'it might just work.'

'I'm headed down Mexico way,' announced McClure. 'I'll be safe as houses thereabouts. Valance won't follow that far.'

'Forty thousand dollars,' mulled Wilkes distracted. The lure of the money overcame his concern over that bounty man. He strode toward the barn doors. 'We'll set to a plan. Hell, yeah, Mexico sounds swell.'

6

The next morning Reno mapped Arrow Town. Of those people he met — middle-agers with suspicion in their eyes — most said little and hurried on. Some, though, did stop to talk. Word, it seemed, had gotten round. A couple muttered cordialities and one woman engaged Reno in a discussion about the death of Sheriff Polk.

Arrow Town's outer regions, accessible by way of cross-streets and alleyways, possessed the same rundown visage as Main Street: denuded properties set alongside rutted roads. Everywhere, cracked boardwalks and aged horses bearing worn-out tack said money stayed squarely on the livestock range.

At the livery, Ben Moses confirmed this.

'Lomax gives nothing to Arrow Town save his thug guns. This place is dying and now the sheriff is killed.' Genuine affection for Polk brought moisture to Ben's eyes. 'He didn't deserve that.' He blinked and said softly then, 'The way I hear it, Valance, neither did Leyton Gifford.'

'No,' returned Reno sombrely. 'Listen, Ben, I'll stay about town for a while yet. You OK to tend the horse?'

The liveryman nodded. He jabbed a hand at the empty stalls. 'It's just your mare now Terry's mount's gone.'

Reno frowned, recalling the events of the previous day.

'I thought that kid left early. Hell, he weren't here when I got the mare from your assistant yesterday.'

Ben looked confused. 'Terry went back the night you touched town,' he muttered. 'That's to say, he got dragged back. A man turned up and beat the boy some.'

Reno's countenance darkened. 'A man — was it that fat thug Wilkes or his partner?'

'No,' intoned Ben, 'it weren't Wilkes

59

or Solomon.' The liveryman shook his head. 'That man who took Terry I've never seen before. He punched the kid out and lashed him up. I've never seen Terry roughed up like that before.'

'He was Brand O?' questioned Reno feeling growing unease.

Ben shook his head. 'I thought he was.' He jabbed a finger at his own left cheek. 'That man had a scar just about there. Now you say it, that feller didn't know where the Brand O was.'

Reno's guts turned. He saw his saddle slung up nearby and he'd soon reached into the bag and pulled out a piece of paper. He'd carried it with him for a heck of years just in case. He unfolded it, worried it might split with age and overuse, but it opened to reveal an ink profile of a wanted man. He pushed the sheet toward Ben.

A minute later Ben nodded. 'That, Mr Valance, is the man what took Terry.'

Reno strode purposefully out of the livery and towards the saloon. William

Vernon McClure was hereabouts. Reno cursed as he walked, staggered by the unbelievable and sickening coincidence in a land this big that a psychopathic killer he'd always kept an eye on had arrived in Seward County at the same time; he'd also slain the only living kin of his beloved wife Anna May.

Reno stopped and spat at the dirt. What motive could there be to slay old Leyton? Still, where Vicious Bill McClure was concerned, there was usually no motive at all.

★ ★ ★

All the ropers and punchers were out on the range. Terry, still in his room, lay on his bed pondering when and how they'd pull off the heist of his step-father. He'd await word from McClure and then, presumably, the scar-faced thug would make some mock assault and take Terry away. Afterwards, he supposed, they'd wait for Sherman to deliver the money to get his beloved boy back.

61

Across the yard, it was business as usual: Albert Foster readying that day's main meal in the log chuck house; Cain and Phillips smoking by the gallows gate with their rifles propped against a fence. Finally, inside the guard's hut, half a dozen hawkers slept off the previous night's long vigil.

McClure, Wilkes and Solomon squatted in the dust just outside Number 1's doorway planning their heist with whispered words.

'I say we bust into the house and get the dollars at the end of a gun,' Solomon growled at length.

McClure threw a despairing gaze skyward. When he looked at Solomon, it was with eyes that showed scathing contempt.

'Were you born mule stupid? That ranch boss is a kind of rich fool who you can't sway by violence. I've seen his sort before — they'd die before opening their strong boxes.' McClure shrugged. 'No, this kidnap way works. Hell, they'll shift mountains to get their kids back.'

Wilkes nodded. 'OK, then. You give us the word.'

'Say, McClure,' said Solomon then. 'What's your first name?'

'Bill,' spat the Missouri man. 'My mama titled me William V. McClure.'

'And the V.,' pressed Solomon, 'that stands for?'

'Vernon,' snarled McClure, 'after my pa but folks in Missouri said it meant something else.'

'Yeah,' said Wilkes, 'what did they reckon?'

McClure smirked. 'They gave me the name Vicious Bill. Yes, sir, it's V for vicious right enough.'

Wilkes grabbed a handful of dust and let it seep to the ground through his fingers. Oh no, he intoned to himself. They'd hooked up with a maniac. Once they'd gotten their hands on the money, they'd part company with McClure at the first opportunity.

* * *

Besides Stan Gorman and Richard Callaghan there were eight other armed locals now standing in the Deep Gulch Saloon. Reno mused on this volunteer force — most pasty-faced and with little in the way of past action behind them. Still, it was a posse nonetheless. Although he'd always ridden and hunted alone, Reno would not do that now. When this ended, these people would still be here and they had to maintain the peace they earned. Reno would head home to White Falls. Who knew? From amongst these men, the settlement's next sheriff might emerge.

Stan Gorman passed round shot glasses of whiskey and Reno sipped at the one proffered to him with contemplative thoughts.

Richard Callaghan finally broke Reno's introspection. 'How'd we do this, Valance? We ride straight to the Brand O?'

'Listen,' Reno drawled. 'There's stuff you should know.'

Ten minutes later and each man in there had some of the details of

64

McClure's blood-dripped past.

Stan Gorman gave a shrug. 'That's settled then: we ride to the Brand O and bring this scar-face in for a hanging.'

'Yeah,' suggested one of the posse men. 'McClure must've shot the sheriff too. Soon as this man's behind bars we'll send for the judge from Dumbarton.'

Voices rose in assent and Reno stilled them with a raised hand.

'I'm certain McClure murdered Leyton,' he said sourly. 'But as for Sheriff Polk . . . well, blasting a man in the open hasn't ever been Vicious Bill's way.'

'Go on,' pressed another man. 'This McClure — you've told us about some of the killings. What about the rest?'

Reno sighed. 'McClure's a kidnapper. He befriends rich people and then steals their kids for money.'

Stan Gorman looked shocked. 'Damn it! He dragged Terry off to the Brand O. Sherman's got a heck of money.'

Reno nodded. 'I'd say he's hatching

some plan for young Terry Lomax sure enough.'

Richard Callaghan shook his head. 'So he'll set to get money off the Brand O by taking Terry off somewhere?'

Reno crossed to the door. 'I'll fetch my pinto. You men saddle up and meet me here in half an hour.'

Reno set to push out through the batwings but Stan Gorman's shout halted him.

'What does McClure do, Valance? I suppose he leaves the kid some place once he's got his hands on the money?'

Reno turned and shook his head. 'He gets the money and leaves what's left of the kid.' He tipped a finger to the brim of his Stetson. 'Not one of those kidnapped kids survived. They all died, gentlemen, in the hell bloodiest ways . . .'

7

Sherman Lomax crossed the yard, his grimace born of the crankiness of the worst sort of lingering hangover and his eyes filled with the venom of a man saddled with a dead wife and wayward son. His mood, that day, was unquenchably angry. When he spoke, his words drilled out through gritted teeth.

'You idle sons of bitches. It's 2 p.m. and you reckon I'll pay you to squat out here all day?'

Wilkes threw a questioning glance at McClure and then all three men inched to their feet.

Solomon shook his head. 'We've not been given orders, boss.'

'Orders?' bellowed Sherman. 'You're like that half-cut, pig stupid boy of mine. So I've got to map it out morning, noon and night have I? Do like all the others do: get out to the range and earn the stinking dollars I pay you.'

'Err . . . yeah,' stammered Wilkes unsure.

Sherman slammed a clenched fist into his other flat-out palm.

'Good,' he barked. 'Now you'll get your hides on to my grass and I won't be paying three scum-idle dogs for nothing.'

Wilkes nodded and glanced again at McClure.

The Missouri outlaw breathed in deeply. He took easy steps up to Lomax and nodded perfunctorily.

'Say, Sherman, I was telling the boys about you.'

Lomax's eyes narrowed and his body shook with anger.

'Who the hell — ' He stopped short and clenched both hands to fists. 'No two bit hireling calls me Sherman. It's goddamn Mr Lomax, you scum, dirt-bag piece of — '

He fell silent owing to one of McClure's massive hands clutching at his jugular. He gurgled, began to turn

68

blue in the face, gasped for breath, both his ageing hands trying uselessly to dislodge the Missouri outlaw's vice-like grip. Finally, as the ranch boss neared blackout, McClure released his hold and Sherman crumpled down on to his knees. He stayed there, coughing and sucking for air.

McClure knelt down and hissed, 'I reckoned you wouldn't tell us the numbers for that safe. I said you'd rather die first.' McClure drew out his knife and set the blade tip against Sherman's temple. 'I'll dig it in right to your brain.'

Terror helped Sherman recover. He got to his feet, his face pale and his eyes wide and fear-filled. He stayed defiant though.

'You're right there. Kill me, scum, but you won't get my money. Only I know the numbers so you can spit in the wind for it.'

McClure grinned. 'I said so.' He cast a winning look at Wilkes and Solomon. 'There, didn't I say it'd be so?'

Wilkes looked nonplussed whilst Solomon threw both arms out in an act of bewilderment.

'So what do we do?'

'We leave Sherman here,' said McClure calmly. 'We take his boy and I'll make Sherman wish he'd been more accommodating.'

Sherman shook his head. 'Leave Terry be. I can't give you the safe numbers. I won't do it!' He stumbled and backed toward the ranch house. A second later, he hurtled across the yard with a screamed, 'Phillips, Cain, help me!'

McClure lurched after Sherman and caught the cattle baron by the collar of his jacket. That done, McClure's drawn gun slammed on to Sherman's head. The ranch boss dropped like a stone, just the softest grunt escaping his lips before he hit the dirt.

McClure scanned fast. The gallows gate guards tore across the yard with rifles to hand. Phillips and Cain, though, didn't have time to use them. McClure, flat palming the hammer of his Colt, sent a slug that struck Phillips full in the chest. An instant later, Phillips crashed to earth with his shirtfront drenched in blood. A second slug hit Cain in the throat, blood spurting from the bullet's entry point and bringing that man down. Cain lay there, life ebbing fast and his body quivering until final and eternal stillness overtook him.

McClure nodded, satisfied. He stepped across to the guards' hut and addressed the now stirred night-hawkers who, clad in underwear, stared back at him with sleep-cloyed eyes.

'Any man steps outside I'll kill the bastard!'

Soon, in the yard again, McClure holstered his gun and made for the ranch house. As the Missouri man strode forward, Solomon and Wilkes sidestepped their former boss and plunged after the scar-faced lunatic. They both knew, as they ran, that they were up to their necks in blood and murder. It was all the way now. Ahead lay only success and Mexico. Alternatively, it was sudden

71

death by gun or what any outlaw feared
— a rawhide way. Yes, they both accepted
grimly: fail, and face a slow choke at a
rope's end.

* ★ ★

Although they rode at a canter, Stan
Gorman struggled. Soon, Reno slowing
the posse, the barkeep shook his head.

'It's a few miles more,' Stan gasped,
'to their border.'

Reno nodded, cursing again that
collision of circumstances that had
brought him to this.

Just fetch Uncle Leyton, Anna May
had ordered. *Bring him here with haste,
Mr Valance, and don't even begin to
think you'll be at your old ways.* She'd
held up their son as he'd departed the
town of White Falls. '*Just you think on
him!*'

'You OK?' asked Callaghan, dragging
Reno out of his musing.

'A year ago,' Reno answered sonorously, 'I wouldn't have thought I'd be

married with a son.'

'Most gunslingers don't,' returned Callaghan. 'It's not the best way to live with a wife and baby in tow.'

Reno shrugged. 'Having none to care for makes a man easy with killing. Not being scared to die gives you the edge.'

Stan Gorman gulped and all of the posse, considering their own demises, had eyes filled with indecision now.

'Don't worry,' Reno reassured, 'We'll all be safe in Arrow Town when this is done.'

'I hope so,' muttered Callaghan sombrely. 'I've a grandchild on the way and I'm sure keen on seeing it.'

* * *

Terry fumbled for his Colt. The first gun blast from the yard had him rushing to look out the window. He saw his stepfather slumped on the ground and panic gripped him. Was Sherman dead? Phillips had definitely perished — his grotesque shape on the ground was skirted by blood. Terry witnessed Cain's demise — the slug to the throat taking that man to the next place.

The kid cursed and rushed to the bedroom door. Rage and worry flooded through him. Damn McClure — he'd vowed there'd be no killing! Accessory to murder flashed through Terry's mind. You'd hang for that, as sure as the man who'd pulled the trigger.

Now, in the hall, Terry's fingers shook as he slid slugs into the pistol's chamber. He'd seen Wilkes and Solomon in the yard. Two drunken hoodlums, for sure, but they wouldn't stand by and see the Brand O boss mistreated and ranch-hands slain like that. They'd assist in bringing down this Missouri psychopath.

Terry reached the arched oak door and dragged it open. He lurched out with his gun levelled.

'You bastard,' he bellowed, drawing a bead on the fast closing McClure. 'One more step and you'll be in hell.'

McClure came to a stop with a

wistful grin playing at his lips. 'But, boy,' he returned, 'we're partners aren't we?'

'Nobody was to die,' Terry screamed. 'You promised that.'

'Ah, well,' drawled McClure, 'it didn't quite work out.'

Terry shook his head. 'You're a murderer and it finishes here.' His finger twitched at the trigger but he didn't fire. A double-click of cocked rifles made him inch his gaze round.

Wilkes and Solomon stood there, carbines primed and aimed straight at him. Terry sighed and lowered his gun hand.

'That's right, kid,' snarled Wilkes. 'Now drop that Colt.'

Terry's guts turned and he let his revolver spill from his grip. Soon, McClure had grabbed up the Colt and hurled it into the distance.

'What now, McClure?' Terry made his voice brave though terror turned his guts. 'You think — '

He didn't finish. McClure's arm

moved fast and the outlaw's gun butt hammered down on to Terry's head. Terry dropped with a groan to lie senseless at the Missouri man's feet.

Wilkes and Solomon hurried across.

'Jeez,' spat Solomon, 'those shots will draw ranch-hands in.'

McClure gave a curt nod. 'Lash the kid to a horse. We're set to the hills.' He smirked. 'I got a shack out there some old feller left me.' He reached down, grabbed a handful of Sherman Lomax's shirt front and hauled the ranch boss to his feet. A couple of backhanders to Sherman's face brought the man round. He moaned against the pain.

'Now listen well,' spat Vicious Bill. 'We're taking your boy and I'll send bits back every couple of days.'

'Please,' Sherman pleaded groggily. 'I'll open the safe. Let Terry alone, I beg you. Take what you want, just leave us alone.'

'Sure you will,' Vicious Bill growled, 'but first you need to get molasses off me.'

More alert now, Sherman's eyes showed his fear and confusion. 'I don't — '

'There's a man in Arrow Town,' hissed Vicious Bill, 'by the name of Valance. I need him dead. Your boy will stay alive if you and your men put an end to Valance.'

McClure released his hold and the ranch boss crumpled to the earth. He dropped down on to his knees and then sprawled on to his back as Vicious Bill applied a boot sole to his chest.

'Get Valance's killing done quick,' said Vicious Bill stepping away then, 'or I'll send Terry's ears tomorrow.'

Sherman dragged himself upright and gave a protracted sob.

'I'll do it,' he cried. 'I'll find a way.'

Vicious Bill hauled himself into the saddle and motioned toward Wilkes and Solomon.

'Please,' Sherman cried, 'keep my boy safe.'

'When Valance is dead,' said McClure softly, 'your boy will be home. There's a shack in the hills north. You bring Valance's corpse and eighty thousand dollars and you get Terry.'

'I'll do it,' said Sherman. 'I'll get someone to finish Valance and I'll be there with the money.'

'Yeah,' McClure shouted. 'That's right, you will.'

A moment later, McClure raked spurs. Soon, the kidnappers and Terry out of view, Sherman dusted himself down and heard horses approaching from the west. Hands were galloping in from the further reaches of the ranch. He needed to think and plan. Soon, men reining up around him, he barked his instructions. But no one listened. He watched as the ranch guards, dressed now, filed out of their sleeping hut and headed to the stabling.

'We're leaving,' said one jerking a thumb at the bodies of Cain and Phillips. 'This isn't safe work, Mr Lomax.'

Soon, left alone in the yard, Sherman watched the last of his ranchmen riding into the distance.

8

In their comfortable home in White Falls, Anna May cradled the baby they'd named Daniel Reno Valance. At the same time, she gave a decided nod at Sheriff Bill Fitz.

Fitz sipped coffee before saying reflectively, 'I'll sure be glad when Reno returns, Anna May.'

She smiled. 'I will too.' She gave a wink then. 'I laid it to him harsh before he left. Letting a man like Mr Valance off the leash for too long is just asking for trouble, Sheriff.'

Fitz looked alarmed. 'He wouldn't — '

'He wouldn't dare,' Anna May cut in. 'He's got too much here to risk it.'

Fitz laid the coffee mug aside and said, 'This uncle of yours — I just didn't know.'

'Uncle Leyton,' returned Anna May with a frown, 'set to the Hills a time ago. He's lived alone up there ever since.'

'And his trade,' inquired Fitz intrigued. 'What does he do?'

'Nothing,' Anna May said stoutly. 'He doesn't need to.'

She explained then: how Leyton Gifford had been in on a gold strike and had gotten out before the hordes struck. With sizeable nuggets in his saddlebag, he'd ridden to find a suitable assay office. An undisclosed sum richer, he'd retired to the Green Coat Hills to live out his life in quiet obscurity.

'He deposited that money?' said Fitz musing on the windfall Anna May and Reno would inherit when old Leyton finally passed on.

'He never trusted banks,' said Anna May. She fixed Sheriff Fitz with a revealing stare. 'He buried it under the floorboards of his shack up in them hills. Anything happens to him I'm to send someone to recover the dollars.'

Fitz sighed and rose to his feet. 'I suppose — '

'Not a chance,' said Anna May impishly. 'I wouldn't let Mr Valance know that. Sheriff, the man's a born follower of money.' She gave another wink. 'What he doesn't know won't hurt him.'

* * *

They all exited the saddle and led their horses up the final stretch of trail to where the wood shack showed under the thick umbrella of trees. It seemed, Wilkes mused, an odd place to site a home. The hill's slope with its colonization of oaks afforded little enough light; the air hung thick with heat and odour, and any form of farming up there would be a struggle. Perhaps whoever owned it panned for gold or silver? The stillness about the shack struck both Wilkes and Solomon then.

'This man what owns it,' grunted Solomon voicing his disquiet. 'Where's he at?'

McClure nodded at a brush clump.

'What's left is in there.'

Max Solomon stopped walking and gasped, 'You killed him?'

'I reckon so,' scoffed McClure. He moved on and approached the shack. A small fenced yard fronted the building and soon, with his horse tethered, McClure unlashed Terry and hauled the kid in through the shack's open door.

'Jeez,' growled Solomon casting a frantic glance at Wilkes. 'What are we doing with this crazy man?'

Wilkes shrugged. 'It's too late now. We're too far in to get out. The only way is to get the dollars old man Lomax pays for Terry and ride the hell away.'

'I'm not setting for Mexico with *him*,' growled Solomon. 'We'd best ride in a whole different way.'

Wilkes shrugged and said in hushed tones, 'We got to settle McClure before he turns on us.'

Solomon gulped. 'I'm not sure, Kyle. That man's so tight-strung. You reckon we'll get us a chance?'

'He's got to sleep, hasn't he?' growled Wilkes. He jabbed a hand at the shack. 'We'll wait on Lomax bringing the money.'

Max Solomon nodded but his look stayed grim.

'Yeah,' he muttered, 'Let's hope that don't take too long.'

* * *

In the Brand O ranch house, Sherman Lomax swallowed whiskey and pondered hard. So deep and troublesome were his thoughts it took repeated rapping on his door to catch his attention. He put the empty glass down and sighed.

'Come in.'

The startled face of the cookie Albert Foster showed. 'God's teeth, Mr Lomax, what's happened? Cain and Phillips are dead.'

Sherman nodded. 'That man McClure killed them. He's kidnapped Terry with the help of Wilkes and Solomon.'

Albert shook his head. When the

83

shooting began, he'd hunkered down in the cookhouse determined not to be involved. He'd been increasingly shocked at Sherman's disintegration and the calibre of men he'd recently taken on. *You've gotten what you deserved*, came to the chuck man's mind but he did not utter it.

'Shall I ride to Arrow Town?' said Albert. 'Call the law?'

'I'd wait a while,' said Sherman firmly. 'McClure, Wilkes and Solomon could still be close.'

Albert gulped and nodded assent. Now he thought about it, he wasn't riding anywhere with the risk of being shot. Albert moved to leave but stopped short when Sherman Lomax spoke again.

'Will you bury those poor men?'

Albert nodded then hurried out.

Still seated at his desk, Sherman dropped his glass, held his head in his hands and wept steadily. For the first time he'd lost his grip on the reins and it seemed like his life careered out of control toward some nightmarish abyss.

With a fire raging in the hearth, they boiled up coffee and Max Solomon heated beans in a pan suspended above the flames.

'Hell,' he muttered. 'That man didn't have much stock.'

'No,' returned Vicious Bill. 'I ate most of it.' He prodded a foot at Terry who, bound by a rope to a chair, sat there silent and sorry looking. 'You OK, kid?'

'What are you going to do to me?' Terry's voice trembled as he spoke. 'Please, I'll get Pa to pay what you want.'

'Too late,' grunted McClure drawing on a cigarette. He blew out a ring of sweet-smelling smoke and chuckled. 'Eighty thousand dollars is what your pa will pay. Still, having Valance dead is worth much more than that.'

Terry mused on that rugged hard as nails quick-draw whom he'd met in the Deep Gulch Saloon a couple of days before.

'Valance is real cool with that Remington,' said the Lomax youngster nervously. 'I'd say that man's a professional killer.' Terry gulped and cursed himself for uttering it. He was desperate and he'd rashly mouthed those words in the hope they'd unsettle the outlaws and persuade them to flee. It didn't work.

McClure drew on his cigarette before saying gruffly, 'In my line you don't want to meet Valance.' He spat at the shack's warped floorboards. 'That, kid, is why your pa's people are going to face him.' McClure sighed. 'I heard say Valance blasted a dog called Buffett from ninety feet. Hell, that there quick-draw shot the man right between the eyes.'

Solomon stepped away from the cooking pan and Wilkes, who'd been gazing distractedly out of the window, turned to appraise McClure with a concerned look.

'That right?' Solomon blustered. 'Valance did that?'

'So I heard,' said McClure drily. 'You know, I never did reckon he'd come after me.' He gave a shrug and nodded towards the blood-spattered bedroom. 'I need sleep. Wake me in a few hours.'

Wilkes, his gaze darting furtively, mumbled, 'Err . . . yeah, sure we will, Bill.'

'First, fat man,' McClure spat, 'corral the horses and bring our rifles in here; I'll stack them in the bedroom with me.'

Wilkes threw a panicked look at Solomon but he said nothing. A moment later, he departed the shack. When, after ten minutes he returned, he'd gotten the carbines cradled in his folded arms.

McClure gestured to the bedroom and Wilkes stepped through and dropped the rifles on to the floor.

'Now your Colts,' growled McClure. 'I aim to wake up.'

Wilkes shrugged and added his pistol to the pile of guns. Soon, Solomon did the same. Finally, as the two Montana men exited, McClure collapsed onto the bed with a loud grunt. Moments later, his sonorous snores breaking the quiet, Wilkes and Solomon swapped fast glances.

Terry's heart pounded in his chest and worry gnawed at his guts. He saw Solomon slowly draw a knife out of his belt. It was clear what they intended to do.

★　★　★

Sherman Lomax walked shakily out of the ranch house as the massed riders eased their mounts into the yard. When all the snorting horses had stilled, the cattle baron noted the rugged man with a star pinned to his vest.

Reno, at the same time, perused the ranch boss before nodding in the direction of the slain Cain and Phillips.

'We ran into some men on the way here. It looks like you're a might short-handed from here on in?'

'That's my business,' barked Sherman. 'I'll get new hirelings. Hell, I always have.'

Reno frowned. 'Perhaps you'll be careful who you choose. I mean, when you take on the likes of Bill McClure.'

Distain and rage showed in Sherman's eyes. He glared at Reno before directing a piercing stare at Richard Callaghan.

'I don't get it. How'd a posse get here so quickly?'

Callaghan shrugged. 'We came looking for McClure. Someone shot Sheriff Polk dead last night. McClure's our suspect.'

Sherman's face drained and he held his gaze down for a while. When he glanced up again he muttered, 'That's a real shame. He was a good old boy, Wendell Polk.'

Reno fought his rage. 'About Bill McClure,' he spat, 'did you even — '

'For God's sake,' Sherman's roar interjected. The cattle baron's eyes burned with anger. 'The man came for a job. I don't know the ins and outs of a cur's ways. He said he was honest.'

'When he came,' Reno went on calmly now, 'it's said he'd gotten Terry

89

lashed to a horse. That didn't set you thinking?'

Sherman looked flustered. 'He said he'd been in Arrow Town,' the ranch boss growled. 'He said Terry had been causing trouble and he wanted to do me a favour by returning the boy.'

Reno's look hardened. 'And now he's took Terry?'

'Yeah,' wailed Sherman. 'He's kidnapped my son and he's helped by them scum dogs Wilkes and Solomon.' Sherman stared forlornly at the corpses of Cain and Phillips. 'Those men tried to help me but it was no good.'

Reno slid out of the saddle and approached the cattle baron.

'How does McClure want it?'

Sherman shrugged and his mind started to work fast. 'He's took Terry to New Mexico,' he lied. He panicked now, fearing if the law knew where Terry was held they'd try to storm the Green Coat Hill, and put the boy's life at risk. I'm to set down there in a month with eighty thousand dollars.'

Reno nodded. McClure had used that tactic before — removing his victim a while to concentrate the mind of the parents before collecting the ransom money and giving the payee instructions on where to find their offspring. Always before they'd ridden on to find a bloody corpse.

'I'd reckon to ride on after them,' said Reno glancing around at the posse men. 'I'd say — '

'I'm not going to New Mexico,' shouted one of the Arrow Town shopkeepers. 'My wife gave me daggers for joining a posse at all. Hell, I'd be lynched in my own kitchen if I went that far.'

A murmur of agreement swelled from the posse.

Sherman Lomax sank to his knees and he covered his face with his hands. A second after, with his body racked with sobs, Lomax howled out, 'Terry. I tried to save you, son. I did my best.'

Reno returned to his horse and had soon mounted up again.

'I'll write the murders of Cain and Phillips down to McClure,' he said. 'They'll join a long list of victims.' He pointed at the two slain men. 'You best get those bodies under earth. They lie there much longer there won't be much left.'

'They'll be under soil by dark,' growled the ranch boss nodding toward Albert Foster who leaned on a shovel by the cookhouse door. A few moments later, to Sherman's relief, the posse moved their mounts toward the gallows gate.

'You, Sheriff,' Sherman screamed as the posse began to exit the compound. 'What's your name?'

'Reno Valance,' sounded across the yard.

'I'll get my boy, Valance,' howled Lomax as the riders left the dust road and took their horses on to the plains. 'No matter what it takes, no matter what it costs. You hear that, Valance? I'll move hell itself to get Terry home.'

'I'll be stopping at the Deep Gulch in

Arrow Town for a few days,' Reno yelled then. 'If there's any news I want to get it.'

'Oh, you'll get it all right,' Sherman muttered softly as he watched them disappear. 'You will *get* it, Mr Reno Valance!'

9

Inside the lamp-lit shack, Terry listened to McClure's deepening breaths with a feeling of elation. Whilst the scar-faced outlaw slept, Kyle Wilkes and Max Solomon ate heartily.

'That man must be dead beat,' Terry said softly. 'I'd reckon him so worn through he'll sleep for hours.'

'Maybe,' Wilkes scoffed between mouthfuls of food. 'What's it to you if he do?'

'You boys,' drawled Terry. 'I know you got in with him when you didn't rightly mean to.'

Max Solomon gave a snort of derision. 'We got in with him? Land's sake, it were you planning to skin your pa of dollars with that scar-faced creature as your partner!'

'I fouled up,' whined Terry. 'You know how Pa and I fight.' Terry's eyes

94

flashed pleadingly. 'If you let me loose I'll see you're rewarded; I'll say McClure forced you to this at gun-point.'

Wilkes shoved his cleared plate aside and wiped his lips with one of his shirtsleeves. He gathered some makings from the pocket of his vest and soon had a cigarette neatly built.

'Your pa won't go for that,' he retorted. 'He saw us ride off with you and McClure. We're marked men.'

'No,' Terry implored. 'We'll say McClure ordered you out with me. I'll make Pa see you were forced to it.'

Solomon ran his mind over the events at the Brand O and then he gave a resolved nod.

'Hell, the kid could be right. We didn't touch Sherman no how; McClure killed Cain and Phillips. We could say that scar-face threatened to slay us unless we went along with it.'

Wilkes puffed on the cigarette and his eyes narrowed.

'We return you,' he said slyly, 'How

much is it worth?'

'Twenty grand,' said Terry excitedly, 'maybe more.'

'Yeah,' Solomon gushed. 'We'll draw the money and — '

' . . . Wish you hadn't messed with Vicious Bill.' McClure stood in the bedroom doorway, a Colt to hand. He shook his head. 'Now, I'm disappointed. I mean, you're my goddamn right-hand men and you up and turn against me.'

Solomon dropped his fork and his face drained of colour. 'We didn't — '

His words choked off as Vicious Bill swung his Colt level and slammed a finger at the trigger. A deafening roar heralded a slug that tore into Solomon's forehead and drove his body off the seat. When Solomon's corpse settled, it rested crumpled and grotesque on the rotting floorboards.

Wilkes froze, the cigarette burning shorter between his fingers. His terror-wracked thoughts screamed at him to run but he just couldn't move. That inertia cost him dear.

Twenty minutes later, now also tethered to a chair, Wilkes struggled against the binding rope.

'OK,' said Vicious Bill drawing a knife from his belt and stepping behind Wilkes. He cast a knowing look at the wide-eyed and watching Terry. 'This is how I done it in Missouri.'

Terry clenched his eyes shut against the vision. However, he couldn't blank the screams. For what seemed an eternity Wilkes emitted guttural howls of agony and he pleaded for an end. When it did cease, Terry looked with horror upon Wilkes's mutilated corpse sagging at its bonds. He felt bile rising in his throat and he gagged against vomit.

At the door, McClure gazed out at the tree-choked vista.

'We best hope your pa don't let me down,' he said without looking round. 'You ask fat man Wilkes there. If he could talk, he'd tell you straight that there's some bad ways to die.'

Reno, seated in the saloon, took a last drink as Stan Gorman arranged towels over his beer pumps. A short while later, a whiskey bottle to hand, Stan slid into a chair opposite.

'That's that then?'

Reno sipped the redeye and nodded. 'I guess so.'

'What'll you do?' Stan pressed, pouring out the whiskey.

Reno shrugged. 'Have Leyton's burial tomorrow and then set home.' He sighed. 'It sticks in my caw though. I mean, McClure was here and I let him slip through my fingers.'

'It's not your fault,' Stan reasoned but then his face paled. 'God knows where Arrow Town goes from here. Our sheriff killed; two decent men slain at the Brand O; Terry took off and maybe . . . ' he trailed off with a curse.

'A time ago,' said Reno earnestly. 'I'd have hunted McClure till the end. Not now, though. I need to get home to

White Falls.' Reno shrugged. 'You'll need a new sheriff.'

Stan sighed. 'Look, bury Leyton and get to your wife and child. We'll get by; we always have.'

Reno rose to his feet and set toward the stairs. He halted before ascending. 'I'm sorry. If I could stay and — '

Stan, silent, stepped away through the rear of the bar.

Reno took a last glance at the deserted saloon. Later, collapsing on to the bed, his last thought was of his wife and son. No, nothing would prolong his stay in Arrow Town.

'As I live and breathe,' he muttered softly before sleep took him, 'I'm going home.'

★ ★ ★

At length, mercifully, McClure dragged the corpses of Solomon and then Kyle Wilkes — still lashed to the chair — through the door. When the psychopath returned, he had a bottle to

99

hand. In no time, McClure tipped whiskey down Terry's throat.

'There,' the killer growled. 'I'd say I shook you some?'

'Yeah' gasped Terry, 'I'm scared enough.'

McClure eased down into a chair and glugged a sizeable measure of the redeye himself.

'Goddamn,' he barked then. 'That old man's bones have gone.' He shook his head. 'What do you reckon, kid?'

'Critters?' mumbled Terry.

McClure shrugged. 'Maybe!' He shook his head. 'Who'd figure Valance would track me to this dog-dirt country.'

'You scared of that man?' Terry baited despite the terror that still churned his guts.

'I don't scare,' raged McClure casting the drained bottle aside and grabbing for his knife. He calmed then. 'I see what you're at, kid, sure I do. Now, you listen. Valance is a mean son of a bitch but he's gotten old. Hell, he's past forty. I'd reckon that's no age for the gunslinger game.'

'He might still be good,' Terry said in hope. 'If he is, how is my pa meant to have him killed?'

'I don't know,' growled McClure struggling to keep his eyelids open. 'You just best hope your pa does.'

A moment later, McClure slumped in the chair and snored. Terry stifled the sobs but couldn't stem the tears. He'd die in that shack, he felt sure. Finally, his weeping finished, his head dropped forward as tiredness overtook him.

10

Sherman awoke with a groan. It felt like red-hot pins pierced his head whilst desert dryness sat in his throat. He forced himself upright in the chair and then blinked against the daylight flooding in through his office window. He struggled to align his sight to the clock hands and when he finally did, he angrily noted the time: 8 a.m.

Up on his feet, Sherman perused his Colt lying on the desktop. He recalled those thoughts the night before and dismissed them forever. Rage beset him now, not desperation. He'd triumph as he'd always done. He'd vanquish any that stood against him. No man — or no man who'd lived past trying — had ever bested Sherman Lomax. He'd rescue his boy Terry and make those three men who'd kidnapped him suffer the agonies of hell.

Firstly, he needed to slay Reno Valance and bring the corpse here to the Brand O. At the window then, Sherman gazed out and saw that the bodies of Cain and Phillips were gone. Albert, as agreed, had put the slain guards into the soil.

Spitting a curse to those ranch-hands who'd deserted him the day before, the ranch boss mused that only one man remained loyal — dear, dependable cookie, Albert Foster.

In no time, out in the yard, Sherman made a decision.

'Albert,' he bellowed as he ran. 'Get my buggy ready. We're set to Dumbarton.'

* * *

McClure yanked out his knife and shook his head.

'I should slice you up,' he growled, 'for setting against me with that pair of snakes.'

Terry gasped as the weapon's serrated blade, still caked in Wilkes's blood, neared his face. A moment later, mercifully, McClure slid the knife into his belt.

'Please,' Terry gasped then. His body trembled ceaselessly despite the tightness of the rope that bound him, whilst sweat wetted his brow. His guts turned and the feeling just got worse. 'Don't kill me,' he begged. 'Don't do it.'

McClure settled into a chair with a curt nod. 'Once your pa shows with my money I'll think about it.'

★ ★ ★

Sheriff Polk's burial took place at 10.30 a.m. Within and about the picket-fenced graveyard, it seemed every resident of Arrow Town crowded. Reno presided on the lowering of the casket. He wished Anna May had been there. She'd have the way with words and the knowledge of the Good Book to deliver a suitable eulogy.

As it was, Reno took off his Stetson and muttered, 'This man Wendell Polk took the badge and served this town nigh on thirty years. He was a good man, an honest man, a brave man. He died in the line of duty and he'll be remembered a hero.'

Ten minutes later, two locals heaped soil into the grave.

Stan nodded at one of the grave fillers who rested on his shovel and looked their way.

'Ralph's opened another plot for Leyton to get laid down.'

Reno nodded and watched as two men lifted up a casket containing Leyton's bones. Once again, Reno said a few words, and with both ceremonies completed, people began to file out of the graveyard. Reno stayed a while musing despondently on the deaths of Polk and Leyton Gifford. When he finally turned to exit the cemetery, he was surprised to see Mary Gorman standing by the picket gate.

She reached into the pocket of her apron and produced the sheet of paper that Polk had previously been in possession of.

'Wendell gave it me the day after you hit town,' Mary said. 'You've some history, Reno Valance.'

Reno shrugged. 'That man I was . . . I don't know him now.'

She turned to leave but hesitated. She smiled weakly and then muttered, 'Thanks anyway.'

'I haven't done a thing,' said Reno with more than a hint of self-loathing.

'The way I see it,' she retorted. 'There wasn't a thing you could have done. Sherman burnt his own fingers with the thugs he's been hiring. As for Wendell Polk . . . well, if you'd known he was on that street facing those curs you'd have been there.'

Reno nodded and proffered a hand. Mary passed over the sheet of paper upon which the exploits of the Hired Ace had been overstated. Reno read it and then shrugged. Then, crumpling the sheet he shoved it into a pocket. 'I'm older now. I don't have — '

'No, Mr Valance,' said Mary edging out through the gate. 'I'm sure if you'd known the sheriff was on that street then Wendell Polk would be alive now.'

She left and Reno set to move. He got a hand on the gate when Mary's words sounded again.

'They'd also be,' she bellowed from the street, 'those curs what killed him, dead at your feet.'

★ ★ ★

They reached Dumbarton just past noon. This large settlement was the perfect site to recruit. Albert brought the buggy to a halt on Main Street and shook his head.

'It's too busy,' he spat. 'It's too darn noisy.'

'Busy means people,' retorted Sherman. 'Where there're people I can hire on.'

'You'll not get forty men today,' growled Albert.

Sherman didn't answer. He climbed down from the buggy's seat and headed up the boardwalk steps. A short while later, he pushed through the batwings of one of Dumbarton's many saloons.

Inside, in a fug of smoke, a crowd of men bunched the long counter and filled the chairs set about at least a dozen tables. Although one man gave Sherman an inquiring stare as he entered, the rest kept at their drinks and paid him no heed.

Sherman shook his head. There was no chance of anyone hearing him above the noise and he hauled out his Schofield and sent a bullet slamming into the ceiling. As plaster and dust rained down, men dragged out their own guns and only a desperate cry from the barkeep prevented someone firing.

'You crazy fool,' bellowed the bartender. 'You want to die?'

'I need men for my ranch,' responded Sherman loudly. 'It's the Brand O. I'll pay top money.'

Silence settled a while until one man stepped forward.

'How much are you offering?'

'One fifty a month, some upfront.'

That rate of pay was unheard of and

it got instant results. Three more men strode out of the crowd.

Sherman grinned, satisfied. 'There's a buggy outside,' he said. 'Get your horses and gear and be ready in an hour.'

'We'll go round the other saloons,' offered one of the men. 'I'd reckon we can pick up a few more out of work ropers. How many men are you looking to take on?'

'Forty,' Sherman returned.

The man's face showed his surprise but, with a shrug, he and the other hired-on men exited through the batwings.

Sherman stepped up to the bar and jabbed a finger at the still scowling barkeep.

'I'll take a whiskey. Make it a double.'

The barkeep delivered the drink and Sherman slapped a hundred dollar bill on the bar.

'That's for the damage as well.'

With the drink to hand, Sherman settled on the raised section where he drank slowly. He felt half satisfied. He'd hired on men to keep the Brand O running, but he still needed a killer.

★ ★ ★

Reno completed the letter with the help of Ben Moses. Ben then read it aloud, and shrugged.

'It's good, Valance. Your wife, I guess, will be pleased.'

'She'll be pleased I wrote it,' returned Reno with a sigh. 'She'll be mad with what it says.'

Ben nodded and passed the letter to his assistant.

'Wheeler's set east later. Tell him to go by White Falls.' Ben sank next to Reno on one of the bales. 'So she'll be angry you won't be coming home yet?'

'Yeah,' drawled Reno. 'It's better to face McClure than Anna May when she's riled.'

Ben chuckled. A moment later, he turned serious.

'What they're saying: you're some big-shot gunslinger?'

Reno nodded. 'That was a lifetime ago, Ben.' He tapped at the deputy sheriff's badge pinned to his chest. 'This is me now.'

Ben shrugged. 'What can you do about things, Reno? McClure's took Terry to New Mexico; Wilkes and Solomon are running gun.'

Reno frowned. 'Sherman will set down there in a month. I guess I could follow.'

Ben shook his head. 'Why? It's likely McClure will kill Terry anyhow. Sure, you might slay three scum dogs but it'll take you time to do it.' He jabbed out a finger. 'You can't take down the world. Go home to White Falls what pays you; keep them safe.'

Reno sighed, but an instant later he leapt up and grabbed the letter from the assistant. 'This won't be needed.'

★　★　★

The prod of a rifle's muzzle brought Albert out of his thoughts. He'd been daydreaming on the seat of the wagon, but now, jolted from his musings, he studied three men on horseback.

One of them, a hard-as-nails looking middle-ager with a wide brimmed hat gave a nod.

'What's happening here, mister?'

By now, the men Sherman Lomax had hired on had assembled about the wagon with their horses and gear and were talking excitedly about the wages offered.

'The boss has hired on,' growled Albert. 'We lost our other men on account of trouble.' Albert reached for some makings and rolled a cigarette. 'Kidnap and killings we've had.' He struck a match and drew on the smoke. 'Yes, sir, kidnap and killings.'

The middle-ager pulled a whiskey bottle from his saddle-bag and proffered it.

'Take a drain of that and tell us more.'

★   ★   ★

In the hotel, Reno agreed one more night's rent of the room. 'I'll set home in the morning,' he informed Stan Gorman. 'But I'd like to get you a sheriff before I go.'

Stan shook his head. 'No one will stand. Sure, a few joined the posse but that's as far at it'll go.'

Reno frowned. 'If Sherman's hired on rough hands before, he'll do it again. You need a young man wearing a badge and willing to bring some order if Arrow Town's got a chance.'

Stan, looking despondent, muttered, 'Yeah, you're right. Maybe we could hire someone on in Dumbarton.'

Reno nodded resolved. 'Then tomorrow I'll go there to get a lawman. I don't want to ride out of here and leave you at the mercy of more gun-wielding thugs.'

11

They rode off, leaving the now inebriated chuck man struggling to stay up on the wagon seat. Down a side street, they found a seedy bar. In there, seated about a table, Rob McKee removed his hat and gestured to the keep.

With whiskey delivered, McKee dispensed the strong fluid and mused on what they'd just heard.

The drink-sodden chuck man Albert had revealed all. There had been violence at the Brand O — Sherman Lomax's son Terry had been kidnapped by three men and two of the ranch guards slain. Later, a posse arrived led by a deputy sheriff called Reno Valance.

Cookie, standing by the chuck hut, had heard it all: Terry taken to New Mexico and Sherman setting there later with eighty thousand dollars.

Right now, in Dumbarton to recruit new hands, Sherman offered crazy money but he could afford it. Hell, Albert had slurred, Sherman's strongbox held greenbacks to the tune of two hundred thousand dollars.

★   ★   ★

'I'm getting ornery with waiting.'

Terry gulped, fearing what was coming next.

'Your pa is pushing me to the edge,' McClure continued angrily. 'I'm not waiting forever.'

'It'll take time,' whined Terry trying to placate the scar-faced murderer. 'You said yourself Valance is good. Pa will need to find the right man to finish the job.'

McClure, his swell of rage quieted, sank back into a chair.

'I can't stay here, mind. Valance is too close and if it goes wrong I don't want to risk being in one place too long.'

Terry, swamped with panic, gasped, 'But you told Pa to deliver Valance's body to — '

'Yeah, yeah,' spat McClure shaking his head. 'The clock's ticking is what I'm saying. Your pa best get some speed on.'

* * *

Sherman, on the buggy seat, hauled Albert upright.

'Jeez,' the ranch boss spat noting the empty whiskey bottle Albert still clutched. 'Where did you get that?'

Albert chuckled, dropped the bottle and then flicked the reins to get the team of two moving. Soon, with the buggy leading the way, fourteen men on horseback set towards the Brand O.

Sherman felt exhilarated. They were a mixed crew for sure: not much to look at but with the buffed-leather skin tone and calloused, scarred hands that spoke of experience in the beef trade. He'd have the ranch back up and running that very evening.

'Bosh,' slurred Albert after they'd gone a few miles. 'You got a lot of men.'

'You can get anything with money,' drawled back Sherman.

Albert shook his head. 'I guesh.'

Sherman glanced back at the line of following riders.

'It's a good day's work,' he said. 'Yes, sir, it's a good day's work indeed.'

The lack of a killer, though, still gnawed at him. Perhaps, amongst this group of new recruits — for the right money — Valance's executioner would emerge!

* * *

In that back-street bar, McKee and his two partners Alf Lassiter and Dane Carter pondered on the possibilities.

'That last job,' Baker growled, 'went bad.'

Rob McKee nodded and sipped at his whiskey. He recounted their abortive attempt at a daylight bank raid.

Firstly, no customers were in the establishment; secondly, the staff had stayed calm and defiant. The three Nebraska men had fled the town empty-handed and bitter.

'This sounds like an easy touch,' proffered Lassiter. 'We ride under nightfall to this ranch and empty the safe.'

'Maybe,' McKee muttered. He mused on what the Brand O chuck man, flushed with redeye, had enthusiastically revealed.

'Those names,' growled Dane Carter at length, 'McClure, Wilkes and Solomon. I don't know any of them.'

'Nor me,' returned McKee. He laid his glass aside. 'I heard once of a feller what kidnaps rich kids, mind.'

'It don't matter, do it?' offered Lassiter. 'They took the kid to New Mexico. We're not headed down there.'

'No,' mumbled McKee, 'like you said, Dane, it's an easy touch.' He tapped the butt of the Colt strapped to his right hip. 'We'll let night set in then ride for the Brand O.'

* * *

Anna May put Daniel into his cot and studied his minute features.

'You get ugly as Pa,' she whispered, 'I won't forgive you.'

She walked over to a chair and dropped into it. A second later, she picked up the Good Book and began to read. Some time later, laying the book aside she sighed.

'Come back, Mr Valance.' She stared into the flickering flame of a kerosene lamp. 'Without you, what will Daniel and I do?'

* * *

Sherman sounded out his new recruits one by one. To a man, they all avowed only to deal with the Brand O beeves. None, they all professed, had much experience behind a gun.

Aggravated, but not surprised, Sherman set back to the ranch house. He'd have to kill Valance himself. He mused on that as he passed the cookhouse. A moment later, he addressed Albert Foster who busied himself at his stove.

'You've got to go to Arrow Town,' said Sherman. 'Albert, you tell Valance to ride here to see me alone.'

'But, Mr Lomax,' growled Albert beginning to sober now after a couple of hours of sleep. 'This meal needs making.'

Night cloaked the ranch complex and Sherman nodded. 'Serve chuck then take a wagon. Tell Valance it's urgent.'

Albert watched the ranch boss leave and he shrugged. OK, then, after the night meal he'd set across the plains. He'd find Valance and deliver the message. With that done, he mused, he'd have a whiskey in the Deep Gulch to ease his return journey.

*　*　*

Having bathed and then taken his meal in the hotel's dining room, Reno made his way to the saloon. An hour later, a couple of whiskeys consumed, he was musing on Anna May and Daniel. Finally, feeling unsettled, he rose from his seat, purchased a bottle of redeye off Stan and strode out through the batwings. He'd go to the livery and share a leaving drink with Ben Moses.

When Reno got to the horse barn, he found Ben sitting on a hay bale polishing a Civil War revolver.

'I reckoned to get this ready just in case,' Ben drawled, looking up. 'When you go we might need to — '

'You'll share a swig or two,' cut in Reno sinking on to an adjacent bale and proffering the bottle.

Ben laid aside the gun and took the whiskey. He swallowed long, handing the bottle back with a gasped, 'It warms the guts.'

Reno quaffed a sizeable drain of the redeye before saying sombrely, 'I sure wish I could do more for Arrow Town.'

Ben shrugged. 'You came to find your wife's uncle. The poor devil's dead and now you've got to go.' A moment later, up on his feet, Ben crossed to a wooden chest lodged against a wall. He bent and lifted the lid, reaching a hand into the casket. When he straightened again, he had a sealed envelope to hand.

'I'd clean forgotten I'd got it,' he drawled. 'Thinking of Leyton's death triggered my mind. It's been in that chest a heck of years.' Ben looked troubled. 'Old Leyton said . . . well, if anything happened to him it was to be opened.'

Reno tore at the envelope and read the paper inside.

'It's Leyton's will,' he intoned then. 'He's left everything to Anna May.'

'Like as not,' returned Ben, 'She's his only relation.'

'But Ben,' gasped Reno, 'he's left fifty thousand dollars.'

Ben grabbed for the whiskey bottle and took another long swig. Laying the bottle aside then, he winked.

'You best get to Dumbarton's bank, Reno, and take that letter with you!'

They reined up on the dark-dressed plains and considered the distant glow of pale light. Squares of white and yellow sat on the horizon and McKee nodded.

'That'll be the Brand O.'

'That boss man must have taken on above a dozen men,' drawled Lassiter. 'That's a lot of guns to set us against.'

'Most of those cow-hands won't be much for shooting,' said McKee dismissively. 'It'll be sweet enough to finish.'

They set to dig spurs but paused as a clatter sounded close by. A moment later, his lit cigarette glowing in the dark, they saw a man trundling along on a wagon.

They moved to intercept.

Albert hauled on the wagon reins as the three riders closed. Soon, their mounts blocking his way, the chuck man shook his head.

'Jeez, fellers, you just about scared me to hell.'

'Where you headed, mister?'

Though Albert couldn't make out the men's features on that night-cloaked plain, he recognized the voice instantly.

'Is it you, boys? Dang, I got me a sore head from that redeye you plied me with in Dumbarton.'

McKee eased his horse closer. 'Hell, it's you, cookie?'

'Yeah,' said Albert with a sigh. 'Now, if you boys don't mind I'll get along.'

'You're sure riding late,' pressed McKee.

Albert shrugged and cast aside his smoke. 'I could say the same of you three.' He shook his head. 'I've been sent to get this Valance feller to ride out to the Brand. It's urgent.'

Carter shifted in the saddle. 'I thought you said that sheriff and a posse came to your boss's place yesterday.'

Albert nodded. 'That's right, they did. I don't know why Mr Lomax wants Valance now.' Albert picked up the team's reins. 'Like I said, I've got to get on. If you want work keep west six miles and you'll be on Brand O land.'

Albert whipped the wagon's team forward and the three outlaws reined their mounts out of the way. Soon, Albert was lost into the inky beyond and McKee shook his head.

'If law's headed this way,' he growled, 'we'd best rob fast.'

Lassiter nodded. 'Yeah, let's ride.'

A second later, with spurs and shouts, they drove their mounts west with a lust for money surging through their veins.

12

In the Deep Gulch saloon, Reno leant against the long counter and sipped slowly on a beer. Deep in thought, it was some moments before he became aware of Stan's voice.

'Let's hope it's over,' drawled the portly hotel man. 'It would be good to get to peace and trade again.'

Reno shrugged. 'I'm sure the thug ways are over.'

Stan's look was inquisitive.

'Tomorrow, Reno, you'll just go to Dumbarton to recruit a sheriff? That'll be it?'

'Yeah,' said Reno. 'I really do have to get home.' A thought struck Reno then and he muttered, 'Hey, Stan, when I first got to Arrow Town you said you didn't know where Leyton got his money.'

'That's right,' said Stan. 'When he

bought stock he had a lot of dollars to spend.'

'It seems Mr Gifford was rich,' returned Reno. 'I'll be asking about that at Dumbarton's bank.'

Stan frowned. 'That's funny. Old Leyton used to curse bankers at every turn. He'd call them thieving dogs and such.'

Reno frowned. 'Maybe he'd problems withdrawing his dollars?'

Stan shrugged and then stepped away to serve another customer.

Reno reached for his glass with troubled thoughts. Logic dictated that Leyton's fifty thousand had been safely ensconced in one of Dumbarton's vaults. Yet, from what Stan had just said, that would be the last place the murdered hill man would have trusted money.

★ ★ ★

They got to the ranch house complex unchallenged. Now, urging their mounts down a track, a voice hailed out of the dark. 'You looking to get took on?'

They reined up as a man on an Appaloosa rode close.

McKee nodded. 'We heard this place is offering good money.'

The man chuckled. 'It sure is. Lomax seems to have more dollars than sense. We'll all make a living here, I'd say.'

McKee pointed toward the gallows gate. 'We'll just ride in then and speak to Lomax?'

The man on the Appaloosa laughed. 'I'd say so. Be quiet, mind. The boys are sleeping against an early start. I'll give up this guard duty soon and get some shut-eye myself.'

They progressed into the deserted yard. Soon, out of the saddle, they perused the ranch house. That Palladian frontage stood in darkness except for one room. Through a window on the ground floor, illuminated by several lamps, they could see a man seated at a desk. If that was Sherman Lomax, McKee mused, he proffered no discernible movement.

'Maybe he's asleep,' drawled Lassiter.

McKee shook his head. 'Come on, let's get it done.'

Fast strides got them to the house. They considered the high arched oak door and McKee groaned. A locked entrance would mean a forced assault through one of the ground floor windows. The noise of shattering glass would definitely alert Sherman Lomax; it might bring ranch-hands out of their slumber to investigate. Once again, blinded by greed, they'd charged headlong toward a robbery without having thought it fully through.

McKee cursed and inched his fingers to the doorknob. A second later, as it moved and the door creaked open, he stifled a cry of triumph.

They stepped in, considering the difficulty of navigating the house's unlit interior. They waited a time, letting their eyes settle to the dark. Finally, they stepped tentatively across a tiled vestibule and into a corridor. Part way along the passage, a yellow glow showed under a closed door.

They gathered outside it and McKee inched his fingers to the handle. He tried it, gasping with elation as it gave way.

Carter and Lassiter drew their guns whilst McKee levered the door open. Then, with curses raging in their minds, they charged into the room.

Inside, stilling as one, they stared, aghast at the dilemma they faced.

Sherman Lomax, still motionless behind his desk, had a Schofield pistol's muzzle lodged in his mouth. His eyes widened as they ran in but he kept the gun trained at his throat.

'Jeez,' growled McKee. 'You won't do it.'

Sherman extracted the gun and placed it on the desktop.

'I've been working up to it. If you boys hadn't stopped by I might just have tripped the trigger.'

Lassiter shook his head.

'Why'd you want to kill yourself? From what we heard, you've money enough.'

'Money?' bellowed Sherman. 'What does money get you but trouble? Have money, you sons of bitches, and there's only hell's time from trying to keep it!' He gave a long sigh. 'Sure, I'm rich enough but you listen. My wife died five months since, all my men have left, and then three fast-draws I took on go and kidnap my boy. What good is money when you're faced with that?'

McKee raised his gun, and used the muzzle to tip back the brim of his hat.

'Jeez,' he said. 'I thought this robbery would go easy.'

Sherman's look darkened. 'Not you dogs as well?'

'I reckon by that,' drawled McKee, 'you won't open the safe?'

'Hell,' Sherman spat. 'Why do you think they took my boy?'

'We'll torture you,' snarled Carter. 'We'll get the numbers.'

'Do your best,' retorted Sherman taking up the Schofield again and placing the muzzle end against his forehead. 'I'll put my brains out before you get close.'

McKee knew they were beaten. He bedded his gun and nodded at the others who soon sheathed their pistols.

'Listen, mister, I can't quite get my head about this.'

Sherman eased the Schofield down and nodded at a whiskey bottle. 'We'll drink some and see what use you boys can be.'

So it evolved, over chat and redeye, that the deal was struck. McKee, Lassiter and Carter would slay Reno Valance when he got to the Brand O. Afterwards, all of them would go to the Green Coat Hills to deliver McClure his money and seal the release of Terry.

'Those scum what took your boy,' drawled Lassiter after handshakes. 'You want us to kill them too?'

'I've got a lot of dollars in that safe,' said Sherman, 'If you kill Valance, save Terry and put McClure, Wilkes and Solomon in hell I'll give you it all.'

McKee nodded. 'It'll be a time yet till that sheriff gets here.' He frowned. 'We haven't eaten today. You got — '

'The chuck hut's out there,' returned Sherman sharply. 'There'll be leftovers enough for you.'

The three outlaws filed out and Sherman reached for a cigar. With this lit, he inhaled the sweet-tasting smoke and felt content for the first time in days. He was in control once more and after this night of carnage he'd never be vulnerable again. Whatever it took, no matter what it cost, he'd get the right people to protect his future interests. Perhaps, by an act of twisted fate, these three who'd set to rob him might be his salvation.

★   ★   ★

With Sherman Lomax's message delivered, Albert sidled to a table clutching a bottle of whiskey.

Reno stared at Stan. 'What do you think he wants?'

Stan shrugged. 'Who knows? What a time to ask you to ride out there!' He re-topped Reno's glass and muttered,

'It's about Terry, I'd wager. You want me to get a posse together?'

Reno swallowed the proffered redeye in one and shook his head. 'He said I had to come alone.'

Stan's look bellowed caution. 'You wouldn't catch me out there on my own.'

'It's OK, Stan,' returned Reno. 'I work best that way.'

With that, Reno exited the saloon and headed to the livery. In no time, with his pinto saddled, he led the mare to the doors.

'Are you crazy, Mr Valance?' growled Ben after a few moments. 'It's dark as hell out there and it isn't safe.'

Reno didn't answer. Out on the night street, he mounted quickly and said, 'I'll be OK.'

With a shout then, Reno raked the mare's flanks with his spurs and they were soon crossing the dark-cloaked plains. Twenty minutes later, the fullest of summer moons lighting his way, Reno let the pinto choose her own pace.

She kept on at a steady pace that got him to Brand O land in a couple of hours. Soon, disquieted by the lack of light from the compound, Reno eased the pinto to a walk. He navigated the track and passed through the gallows gate. He halted the mare then, his senses wire-tight, alert to danger.

An unerring stagnancy beset the complex — house and huts in silent repose. All was stillness and dark. It was too subdued.

Reno inched a hand to his gun and set to slide out of the saddle.

A voice hailed him from out of the unlit reaches of the yard.

'Thank God, Valance, you're here.'

Reno shook his head. 'Lomax — is that you?'

Sherman showed in the ranch house doorway brandishing a lamp. By the glow of that, Reno saw the cattle baron beckoning with his free hand.

'Tie up your horse, Valance. Come in and we'll share a drink or two while we talk.'

'I take it,' Reno growled, 'this is about your boy?'

'Yeah,' returned Lomax, 'but it'd be best if we shared a whiskey to discuss it.'

Reno levelled the Remington, sensing something was wrong.

Lomax called again, his voice louder now and insistent. 'Damn it, Valance, get in here to talk.'

'We'll talk out here,' Reno barked. 'You hear me, Lomax, I don't — '

A gun's bellow drove him out of the saddle. A second later, that sent slug shredding the air above his skittered horse, Reno hit the dirt with a spat curse. He grabbed the pinto's reins and stilled the beast, knowing a second attempt would come. When it did — a flame flash left and a demonic bellow as a bullet hurtled his way — he slammed down on to his stomach and returned fire.

Soon, splintering glass and a man's cursed invective told him he'd missed. Reno stayed prone, easing back the

Remington's hammer and waiting for his chance. When it came — a scuffling noise as the shooter moved — Reno set to exact fatal revenge. He'd gotten up to his knees, seething certainty in his mind, when a blast from the ranch house had him face down in the dirt again.

'Goddamn it,' Reno spat. He lurched for bullets out of his belt to replenish his gun when all hell broke loose.

Slug after slug dissected the space over Reno's prone form. For the longest minutes then, a wrath of noise shattered that night-cloaked yard as bullets tore towards the man called the Ace. Reno flattened his body until he tasted soil. Finally, though, when a slug spat up dirt inches from his head, he lurched up to his feet and blasted as he ran.

He tore forward, swinging the Remington in an arc, that six-gun belting out slugs and getting results. The ranch house door slammed shut and Reno dropped to the ground again with a thankful sigh. He could concentrate his efforts on the would-be killer in the yard.

Now, silence set about the quadrant again, Reno strained his ears for noise. It soon came — logs rolling, preceding a venomous curse. When that commotion died, Reno prepared. The assassin's next shot, he vowed, would be the last.

When flame streaked in the dark, Reno had his man. He sent two slugs and then nodded, satisfied. Soon, confirmation sounded.

'I'm hit,' a pained voice gasped. 'Rob, Alf, help me.' He wailed on a while, imploring those others to come to his aid.

They didn't, though. When the cries subsided, Reno crossed the yard. Soon, lighting a match, he perused a dead man. He lay by a woodpile, hands clutching at his guts. Snuffing the match, Reno whistled to the mare and she trotted across. He climbed back into the saddle and set to leave. But a noise across the yard stilled him.

'What the hell's going on?' a voice

138

bellowed out. 'We're trying to sleep. Who's doing the shooting?'

Reno shook his head. 'Who are you?'

'The name's Naylor. I got took on today. The rest of the boys joined up at the same time.' Naylor paused before yelling, 'Who the hell are you?'

'I'm a deputy sheriff,' Reno answered. 'I'd get in your hut if you boys want to stay out of this.'

After a short pause, Naylor barked, 'OK, but our guns are primed in case any seek to shoot at us.'

A door slammed shut and Reno satisfied himself that the ranch-hands were in their sleeping quarters and safe.

He'd resolved something else as well: once, in his gun-slinger years, he'd have persisted here and fought on to the end. Instead, he'd set to Arrow Town and summon out the posse Stan and Ben had cautioned him to take along in the first place.

'I'll return for you, Lomax,' Reno roared. 'You brought me here to have me killed and I'll settle that.'

A moment later, a ranch house window burst open with a tinkling of glass and Lomax's desperate words cried out.

'They've got me hostage, Valance. God alive, help me.'

'Who's got you?' Reno roared. 'Is McClure in there?'

'Damn it, Valance,' howled Lomax. 'He's in New Mexico with Terry. I told you that. These are partners of his. I had nothing to do with this.'

Reno didn't wait to hear more. He urged the pinto into a headlong gallop across the yard and through the gallows gate. He kept low as he rode, the Remington primed and ready to fire. No more shots came. Soon, he made the parched grass of the plains and drove his horse at full speed toward Arrow Town.

Sherman Lomax's words followed him as he departed.

'They'll kill me, Valance,' the ranch boss's pitiful wail came. 'How can you sleep at night if you leave me to die?'

140

13

McClure placed a kerosene lamp on the table then stepped towards Terry. The Missouri miscreant clutched that death knife with its serrated blade gleaming.

Terry gasped, the feeling of sickness in his stomach like nothing he'd ever known. An instant later, any strength drained out of him. He was to die in the hideous manner of Wilkes. That man had endured for half an hour. Terry knew in his heart he wouldn't survive for that long. He willed McClure just to cut his throat. That, at least, would be a painful but swift death. Shutting his eyes, and whimpering, Terry waited for the pain.

It didn't come. Suddenly, unexpectedly, the rope binding him loosed and Terry felt a grip on his arm. A second later, dragged up on to his feet, he stood trembling before the scar-faced killer.

'I've waited enough,' spat McClure. 'We're set to your pa and I'll show him what I think.'

'Pa will pay,' cried Terry, wide-eyed and fixing the outlaw with a convincing look. 'Whatever you want you'll get.'

'I wanted Valance dead,' snarled McClure sliding the knife into his belt. 'It looks like your pa let me down.'

'He would have tried,' protested Terry desperately. 'Until we get to the Brand we just won't know.'

McClure nodded. 'I'm getting crazy for that money.' He stepped to one side and then glanced down as his weight set one of the floorboards creaking. Dropping to his knees, McClure worked the failing plank loose.

'This shack's falling apart,' he grumbled. He dragged the loose plank up with a smirk. 'Hell, catch your foot and you'd likely get hurt.' He hurled the board at a window and it exited to an explosion of shattered glass. He stood up, not noticing the dust-coated sackcloth bag lodged in the space under the floor.

'Now,' he said with venom, 'you and me ride.'

Outside, with McClure carrying a lamp against the darkness, they progressed first to the corral and then the barn. Soon, with their mounts saddled, they led the horses away.

Half-an-hour later, reaching the grass-land below the hills, McClure growled, 'Don't try to escape. Goddamn it, I'll put you in hell before you get five yards.'

'No way,' retorted Terry triumphantly. 'This will end well for all of us.'

★ ★ ★

In the yard now, with McKee holding a lamp, they studied the cadaver of Dane Carter.

'Goddamn it,' barked Sherman, 'it's all gone wrong!'

'I'd reckon so,' growled Lassiter. 'Dane wasted so.'

'Not that,' Sherman snarled. 'Valance is still alive.'

McKee put the lamp down and shook his head. 'That man is useful with a gun. I'd say we need to change the deal.'

Sherman's face showed his growing rage. 'You dog, I'll — '

'You'll do what I say,' returned McKee calmly. 'You're not in much of a position to call the shots.'

'I already told you,' spat Sherman, 'I'm not opening that safe. I'm not scared to die.'

'We'll all get out of this ahead,' returned McKee, his quick mind having weighed it all up. 'Those three men what took your boy — did any of them know Valance?'

Sherman shrugged. 'Wilkes and Solomon have been in town enough. They could have met him. As for McClure — God knows.'

McKee nodded. 'We haven't got time to worry. An hour or so there'll be a posse hitting this spread and we best be gone.'

'What're you saying, Rob?' pressed Lassiter.

'We'll lash Dane over his horse and cover him with a blanket.' McKee pictured Valance's thickset frame from the slug exchange earlier. 'That lawman was about six feet tall, say a couple of hundred pounds. The dead Dane Carter wasn't far off that. When we get in them hills,' he growled, 'we'll make out Dane's body is Valance and you had him killed like you agreed.'

Sherman's angry mood settled some. 'Go on.'

'Before they get the blanket off we'll blast them,' McKee went on. 'You'll have the boy, and me and Alf we'll be gone.'

'But Valance?' Sherman protested. 'What do I — ?'

'That's your problem,' interrupted McKee. 'You told that lawman you'd been taken hostage — that should save your neck. By the way, that eighty thousand dollars you'd set to pay McClure. That's our pay for saving your boy.'

Sherman felt uneasy but McKee's

145

proposal seemed the only way out of an increasingly desperate situation.

'Can I trust you?' the ranch boss snapped. 'What if I get those dollars and you blast me on the way to the hills?

'Why would we do that?' McKee grinned, 'when we'll set this way again in a few months, when it all settles, we'll ride here to kill Valance. Then, Lomax, you'll pay us a heck of money.'

Sherman nodded. 'OK. You wait here.' He strode towards the ranch house and Lassiter pinned McKee with a look of disbelief.

'You sure about this, Rob?'

'Stop squawking,' spat McKee. 'While Lomax gets them dollars we'll get Dane lashed; you lead his horse when we ride.'

Lassiter nodded. 'Hell, Rob, we set against that man called Valance and we lost Dane doing it. Now, you're saying we got to face three fellers?'

'Don't worry,' said McKee. 'It'll be different up there. We'll have the whip hand.' McKee's eyes narrowed. 'Just think, Alf, if we pull this off we'll never need to rob again.'

★ ★ ★

They stopped suddenly. There, on the pitch-black plains, they waited and listened. A coyote wailed in the coal-dark distance; a hawk's cry replied. Somewhere nearby, a scratching in the grass blades told them a rabbit ran for cover.

'What is it?' Terry hissed after several minutes had passed.

'I'm not sure,' growled McClure. 'I just got a notion I heard a horse riding fast.'

'As like as not,' returned Terry matter-of-factly. 'You always get Brand men riding back from town.'

'What — this late?'

'Sure,' said Terry. 'Some nights Wilkes and Solomon wouldn't leave the saloon till the early hours.'

The Missouri miscreant mused on it all. Brand men riding the plains suggested normality. If so, it meant the

147

slaying of Cain and Phillips hadn't reached the law but it also implied the survival of Reno Valance. Still, needs must, McClure decided. Valance would have to wait. Eighty thousand dollars that Sherman Lomax would pay to retrieve his son sat top of the agenda. Get the money, McClure resolved to himself, then lie low for a few months before returning to kill Valance. He might even get more money off Lomax and his half-wit boy.

Terry's anxiousness to be home sounded in his voice. 'Well, are we headed to the Brand O or what?'

'Yeah,' growled McClure with a hidden nod. 'But we'll go slow and easy. I'm not about to be jumped in the dark.'

*   *   *

Reno thundered his mount into Arrow Town. With the pinto tethered, he got into the Deep Gulch as the clock struck midnight. Soon, with the saloon's noise quelled, men listened as Reno described the events at the Brand O.

Albert Foster, still nursing the whiskey bottle, resolved to sleep in town. The Brand O spelt trouble and Albert wanted none of it. He slunk off, set to slumber in the wagon.

Whilst the Brand O chuck man pushed his way out through the swing doors, Richard Callaghan rose from his seat.

'If you want a posse we'll do it. I'm not keen on riding at night to help Sherman Lomax but if you say it's right, so be it.'

A murmur of concerned voices rolled about the saloon. When that subsided, another man shook his head.

'It's been nothing but death and trouble about Brand O for months. Hell, as for Sherman pining for his lost son it don't sit right. He beat that boy with a birch at every turn.'

'It don't sit right with me either,' said Reno. 'I'm sure Lomax set to have me killed.' He ran his gaze about the tense faces in the Deep Gulch. 'As it stands, Sherman Lomax is held hostage and I aim to get the man safe. Afterwards, well, Sherman's got some explaining to do.'

Stan shrugged. 'If we do ride with you, Reno, how many do we face out at the Brand O?'

'Like I said,' Reno went on, 'I killed one of them. Before that man died he yelled out the names of two others.'

Stan put down a cloth and nodded. 'I'll get my horse ready and we'll have a posse together as quick as you like.'

Gradually, the men began to disperse. A few complained, but it appeared all the participants of the first posse would ride again. Even the one whose wife had been so resistant agreed.

'God knows what I'll tell her,' he mumbled as he pushed out through the batwings. 'She's been at me so much that getting killed on this posse might give my ears a rest!'

14

'This is bad,' spat McClure as the unmistakable drum of hoof beats broke the quiet. 'If it's a posse it might get hot!'

Terry shuddered. McClure was mad; he wouldn't just submit. He'd die blasting those that sought to take him and more than likely he'd slay his hostage in the process. Terry dropped a hand to where his Colt should have been. He was at the mercy of circumstance or McClure's crazy temperament.

'Just keep your mouth shut,' growled the Missouri miscreant. 'I might get us out of it.'

In no time, Naylor and the rest of the Brand O evacuees reined to a halt. They tried, by what the moonlight allowed, to take in this questionable looking man and the kid with him.

'Say, mister,' said Naylor jabbing a finger at McClure. 'You're set towards the Brand O; I wouldn't bother.'

McClure shook his head. 'Me and the boy is strangers hereabouts; we're just trying to find a spot to rest our heads.'

Terry seethed but he kept quiet. He wanted to shout out; he wanted to scream for help and tell these dozen riders to shoot at will and put McClure out of this world. He couldn't do it. He gulped down his urge and hung his head in desperation and shame.

'We're set to Arrow Town,' Naylor said curtly. 'We'll bed down there and head to Dumbarton tomorrow.'

McClure shrugged. 'Those names mean nothing to us.' He gave a forced grin. 'What would you boys reckon to be best?'

'There's been a killing at the Brand O,' another man proffered. Terry's guts lurched but he was quickly reassured as the man added, 'Three fellers turned up and then a deputy sheriff showed.

152

That lawman blasted one of those men and then rode away.'

McClure bristled. 'A lawman you say. What was his name?'

The man thought hard. 'That man,' he said a moment later, 'gave the name Valance.'

McClure kept his rage and surprise hidden. Valance now rode behind a badge. More importantly, he lived still. Exactly whom the famed gunslinger known as the Ace had slain at the Brand O was of no concern. Valance must have returned to Arrow Town.

'That ranch boss,' said McClure then, 'what happened to him?'

Naylor shrugged. 'We don't know. They rode out before we left and they took Lomax and that dead man with them.'

McClure pondered the possibilities. Finally, he said, 'We'll set to those hills. We're not up for shooting and such.'

Naylor nodded. He dragged his horse about and shouted, 'Come on, then. We'll push on.'

As the massed riders drove their mounts across the ebony-coated grassland, McClure and Terry hauled their horses about and set back to the Green Coat Hills. On those occasions that Terry tried to slow his horse he found McClure close.

'Keep up, boy,' hissed the Missouri outlaw at length. 'If you don't, so help me, I'll spread your brains over this land.'

Terry raked spurs then. This living nightmare continued. *When*, he cried in his head, *would it end?*

*   *   *

Clouds had smothered the moon when McKee, Lassiter and Sherman urged their mounts into the Green Coat foothills. They rode on a while, taking a stony trail through the trees. Gradually, as the path steepened and twisted between those towering oaks, they all dismounted and progressed on foot.

Lassiter, leading his own horse and

154

the mustang bearing the body of Dane Carter, gave out a curse as he stumbled in the dark.

'This isn't safe,' he growled. 'I can't see a damn thing.'

'Shut it,' hissed McKee. They moved on, taking the final yards to the crest of the incline with increasing concern. Every laboured step seemed sure to herald their approach — twigs snapping underfoot and their boots dislodging stones that clattered away down the trail. New noise erupted then: the explosive cries of horses that made a mockery of their surreptitious approach.

Amazingly, no bellowing gunfire sounded and they stood on the plateau trying to focus on the blur of structures ahead.

'Over there,' said McKee. A second later, certain those in the shack had heard their approach he bellowed out, 'You hear me, McClure? We done killed Valance and brought his body!'

They waited but an intense quiet settled over the plateau. The horses corralled beside the shack quieted now and save for sporadic critter call they heard nothing.

Sherman began to tremble before howling, 'Jeez, Terry?'

He lurched forward, evading McKee's restraining lunge and quickly reaching the shack door. A moment later, he dragged the door open and scanned inside. In no time, mapping the interior with his hands, he located a lamp and matches and a yellow glow confirmed the truth. The shack was empty. He stumbled from room to room, at one point cursing furiously as his foot slipped into a gap in the floor. He extricated his foot from the hole before crying out through the front door.

'There's no one here; it's deserted.'

McKee and Lassiter soon appeared, McKee clutching the wad of dollars he'd extracted from the saddle-bag of Sherman's horse.

'That's good news,' he said with a grin. 'We've got our money and we'll live to spend it.'

'You bastards,' howled Sherman. He held still then, the muzzle of McKee's Colt pressed between his eyes.

'Shut it, Lomax, unless you want to die!'

Sherman gulped but his rage showed in his eyes. 'Take it then,' he barked. 'You've not done what's been agreed and that eighty thousand will be all you get. Kill me if that's your choice. Like I said, I'm not scared.'

McKee gave a sigh. 'I can't make you out,' he drawled. 'There's been death and hell about you but you're still fighting.'

Sherman shrugged. 'I just want my boy safe. Ride off and I'll search for Terry alone.'

Lassiter turned to leave but McKee put out a blocking arm. 'Stay it, Alf, I've got to think.' A moment later, McKee muttered, 'It just don't add up.' He led the way out to the corral and Sherman's lamp illuminated two quarter horses and a sorrel. 'If they've gone, what are those beasts doing there?'

Sherman shrugged. 'Maybe they got hold of other horses?'

McKee sighed and turned to Lassiter. 'I want the rest of this ranchman's money and it'll mean ending this all tonight.'

Lassiter looked appalled. 'No, Rob, this is madness.'

'We can't do anything about your boy, Lomax,' McKee growled at Sherman. 'Them scum have taken him some place and I'm not wasting time to find out where.' McKee shrugged. 'As for Valance, well, we could settle that for what's in your safe.'

'No,' Lassiter howled at that. 'That man's too good with a gun. God alive, we tried to jump him from the shadows and Dane's dead. We'd best leave Valance alone.'

'That money,' Sherman added with a spat curse, 'was for killing all the kidnappers and Valance and rescuing Terry.'

'Things change,' drawled McKee. 'There's only Valance left and he'll be set about now to the Brand O.'

'Yeah,' Sherman snapped, 'to rescue

me from you two.'

'No,' McKee responded with a smirk, 'to take you in for conspiracy to murder.'

Sherman's blood surged. 'But,' he spat. 'You said — '

'I said he'd believe you'd been taken hostage,' growled McKee. 'I lied. That man pinned you true enough. You'll swing, Lomax, and that's the end of it.'

Sherman gulped. Valance, for sure, would be on Brand O land even now. He'd find the spread abandoned of people, of course. If McKee was right, Valance would not rest at that. He'd hunt on. He'd seek his prey and one Sherman Lomax would face the harshest justice. Sherman saw it all starkly then. His life swung in the balance. Valance's death, though not a cast-iron certainty, might go some way to saving the ranch boss's neck.

'Please,' Sherman wailed. 'What can we do?'

'This place Arrow Town,' pressed McKee. 'How far is it?'

'Ten miles,' returned Sherman glumly. 'But it'll be hours till Valance and the posse get back there.'

'That's time enough,' said McKee, 'to find a killing site. When Valance is dead, we ride to get your money.'

They dragged Carter's corpse off his mount and drove it and the three other horses from the corral down the trail. Soon, they began the descent themselves. Sherman walked with a heavy heart. He had no hands to tend his herds; Terry remained in the clutches of McClure and those two Montana men. Lastly, McKee and Lassiter, if they succeeded in slaying Valance, would bankrupt the Brand O. As they reached the grassland, got into the saddle and then rode, Sherman planned. Valance needed to die but so too McKee and Lassiter. Somehow, in Arrow Town's night-blackened streets, Sherman had to engineer his survival.

15

It seemed an age before the posse had gathered on Main Street and the group was ready to ride.

Reno, aggravated by the delay, hauled himself up on to the pinto with an annoyed grunt.

'Right then,' he bellowed out, 'We'll set to — '

A drum of hoof beats stilled his words. Horses galloped in fast from the town's western edge. In no time, posse men grabbed for their guns. Reno stayed on his pinto but dragged up his Remington and levelled it into the darkness.

Soon, the mounted group slowed, and Reno eased his finger off the trigger. He kept the Remington to hand, though, determined to be ready if the need arose.

When the riders showed — a mass of

men halting their mounts outside the Deep Gulch Hotel — Reno mused on this late-hour entry to Arrow Town.

A nerve-shredded storekeeper beat him to it. Elias Jones, jumpy at the best of times, slammed a finger to his Winchester's trigger and sent a slug that sped past Naylor's ear.

'Jeez,' Naylor cursed. 'What the hell are you shooting for?'

Reno recognized the voice. 'Stay your guns,' he bellowed, 'it's men from the Brand O.'

'Not any more,' Naylor barked. 'We've left that ranch and we figured on spending a night in town.'

Reno holstered the Remington and shook his head. 'It's OK. None will fire at you now.'

In no time, with Naylor and those that rode with him out of the saddle and hitching their horses, Reno slid off the pinto.

'You've deserted Sherman?'

'Deserted,' Naylor scoffed. 'After you left, Valance, so did we. Lomax might pay stupid money but I didn't get took on to get killed.' He shrugged. 'You and this posse riding to the Brand O?'

Reno nodded. 'I killed one of those hostage takers but the other two have got Sherman.'

Naylor spat at the street. 'If that's so,' he said curtly, 'you'll not find them at night on these plains.'

Reno's guts turned. 'They've gone?'

'They saddled up with Lomax,' returned Naylor, 'and they took that corpse as well.'

Richard Callaghan strode down from the boardwalk.

'This is stupid, Valance. Why risk our lives in the dark when Sherman's gone?'

A murmur of assent broke from the rest of the posse. When this quieted, Reno weighed it all up. Sherman Lomax, it seemed, kidnapped like his son and also bound for New Mexico, probably sealed his death by a refusal to open his safe. What good all that wealth, Reno mused, if you died trying to protect it.

'What'll happen with the Brand O?' he voiced to Callaghan then. 'Did Sherman have siblings?'

Callaghan shook his head. 'No, he was an only child. We'll have to write to the governor to make a decision.' He shrugged. 'It's likely the state will take possession of the land.'

Reno sighed. 'OK. There's no point in riding out.' He swung out of the saddle and led the pinto towards the livery.

Stan Gorman had exited the saloon and stood on the boardwalk. He'd heard enough of the conversation to make a decision. He jabbed a hand at Naylor.

'I've got plenty of empty rooms. You and those other fellers can have accommodation and food at a reason-able price.'

Naylor nodded. 'We'll get our horses corralled with the livery and then we'll settle in.'

Half an hour later, sinking into a seat in the saloon and fixing Stan with a despondent look, Reno gave a curse.

'It looks like it's all finished with.'

Stan smiled and produced another bottle of redeye. 'It's for the best, Reno. Drink this and then get some sleep; you've a ride to Dumbarton tomorrow before you set for home.'

Reno swigged out of the bottle. As the redeye burned, he vowed to himself: one day, he'd wreak deadly justice upon that demented Missouri miscreant known as Vicious Bill.

★ ★ ★

McClure grabbed at Terry's reins again and brought both their mounts to a halt.

'Jeez,' he spat. 'It's more goddamn riders.'

Terry heard it then: a drumbeat of iron shoes that said several horses approached.

'This place is crazy,' growled McClure, 'it's as late as hell and it seems the whole world is in the saddle.'

'It's got to be the posse,' cried Terry overcome by panic. 'Please don't — '

'Lash that tongue,' McClure snapped. The Missouri man mused on it all before shaking his head. 'I'd reckon not. Valance is set to the ranch. Whoever this is comes at us from the hills. It's got to be your pa and those men Valance swapped slugs with.'

Terry's guts lurched and then something else struck him. 'Pa,' he gasped, that word layered with both hope and worry, 'he set to the hills to bring you the money. That's good, isn't it?'

'He didn't kill Valance,' hissed McClure. 'He let me down.' McClure dragged a rifle from its saddle berth. He cocked the weapon with a growled, 'No one fails Vicious Bill.'

Terry shook his head. 'You can't — ' He broke off, tracking the drumming intensity of galloping hoofs. Whoever rode closed fast and would be there in an instant. Terry had to act now before the Missouri bastard loosed off a slug.

Lurching out of the saddle, the kid

threw himself into McClure. Half the Missouri man's weight and age, that discrepancy didn't matter. The speed and suddenness of Terry's impact drove McClure from his horse. Howling then, with his finger slipping at the trigger and sending a bullet skyward, the Missouri psychopath toppled to earth. He lost his grip of his rifle as he plunged, but both his death-soiled hands got a grip of Terry's shirt.

They slammed on to the dirt together, McClure cursing and Terry emitting an agonized wail. A second later, freeing one of his hands, McClure clenched it into a fist that he delivered to Terry with unrestrained fury.

Soon, McClure's punches rained in. With the kid screaming, each fist strike slamming the life out of him, he felt blood flooding his mouth and his eyes closing. Still the assault came — hammer blows to Terry's head and midriff to the point where he knew death was close.

'Oh, God,' he gasped as he felt his

life force failing. Then he succumbed, laying there to await the final and fatal blows.

They didn't come. Bellowed words stayed McClure's punches and the miscreant climbed to his feet.

'Go for a gun,' growled a voice out of the dark, 'you'll get a slug in the head.'

McClure sighed. A moment later, reaching down with one of his huge hands, he dragged Terry upright.

'This kid's OK. We was just messing.'

McKee and Lassiter urged their horses forward. Both had carbines to hand. Close behind, a silent Sherman showed.

A second later, though, Sherman dropped reins and shook his head. 'Oh, God, Terry, I'm so sorry!' He made to exit the saddle but McKee threw out a blocking arm.

'Stay there, Lomax, till we got the whip hand of this.'

'I'm OK, Pa,' said Terry weakly. 'This man beat me some but I made it through.'

168

'I came for you, boy,' Sherman yelled. 'You must've known your pa wouldn't let you down.'

'Shut that talk,' growled McKee then. He urged his mount on and jabbed his rifle at McClure. 'Slide out your Colt, big man.' He gave a chuckle. 'I swear to God I'll blast you into tomorrow if you play it funny.'

McClure shook his head. 'I could — '

'No,' spat Lassiter. 'You could take out one of us if you're like lightning but you'll die by trying it.'

McClure, fear gripping at him for the first time in years, inched a hand down and tossed over his gun. It fell to earth with a thump and the Missouri man knew his only weapon now was words.

'Listen, fellers,' he whined. 'You've got it all wrong.'

'Got it *wrong*, McClure?' Sherman screamed. 'They've got nothing wrong. You're a murdering, kidnapping son of a bitch and you'll choke on rawhide for it.'

'But your boy made me do it,'

returned McClure making his voice tremulous. 'He said we'd fleece you with this kidnapping. He said he'd read about such goings on. I didn't want no part of it but — '

'No!' Terry howled. 'It's not true, Pa. McClure wanted it so. He said he'd done this kidnapping before. He killed Cain and Phillips so he'll hang for that and then he killed — '

McClure stopped Terry with a back-handed slap but the click of McKee's cocked carbine stopped a further blow.

McKee shook his head before snarling, 'You're as dead as they come, McClure.' Something struck him then and he said, 'Say, scar-face, where's those two fellers who helped you steal the kid?'

'Yeah,' growled Lassiter. 'We saw their horses up at that hill shack. Where are they, McClure?'

'They're both dead,' Terry cried through swollen lips. 'He shot Solomon and tortured Wilkes.

'Jeez,' growled McKee. 'McClure, I do swear, you're the maddest piece of humanity I ever did come across.'

McClure emitted a protracted sigh. Cornered as he was, with possible death close, he decided to be honest.

'OK. I set to the Brand O and kidnapped the boy. That kid didn't say no to it and that's the truth. He wanted twenty thousand dollars to leave his pa. The kid was all up for it.'

Sherman gasped and muttered, 'Terry, say it's not true.'

Terry stayed quiet and McClure went on, 'Wilkes and Solomon wanted in on the deal. They died because they set to kill me. I mean, any man would do the same.'

'Go on,' growled McKee, 'tell us all.'

'Sherman there,' spat McClure, 'he agreed to have Valance killed. From what I hear he didn't get too far with that.'

'No,' Lassiter barked. 'Valance killed Dane Carter.'

McClure nodded. 'That's as like as

171

not; Valance is the best quick-draw I ever heard of.' The Missouri miscreant shook his head. 'Why'd Valance set against you boys anyhow?'

'Lomax agreed a fee for us to ambush him,' said McKee uneasily, 'then to kill you, Wilkes and Solomon.'

'How much,' McClure snapped, 'did Sherman there offer you?'

'What's in the safe,' answered Lassiter. 'He said close on a quarter million dollars.'

'There's more.' Sherman pushed his horse forward and slid out of the saddle. He felt despair at Terry's attempts to get away but he still hugged the kid. Then, he said firmly, 'There isn't one of us here who wouldn't hang for what he's done. Truth is we're up to our necks and the only way out is to stick together.'

'What are you saying now?' said Lassiter derisively.

'There's a heck of dollars in my safe. That can be split between you if you let me and Terry live.' Sherman paused before adding drily, 'Valance has still got to die. If he lives, we'll all hang for what we've done.'

'I'm up for that,' said McClure. 'All I want is that quick-draw in the dirt.'

'All we've done can stay hidden,' Sherman persisted. 'Arrow Town's sheriff's dead and I own this county. Only Valance stands in our way.' Sherman sighed. 'Besides, he knows who we all are.'

Lassiter shook his head. 'He don't — ' He stopped suddenly and recalled Dane Carter's dying cries at the Brand O. 'Jeez,' he exploded. 'Dane shouted our names. Valance will come after us unless we kill him.'

McClure gave a snort of laughter. 'Who the hell are you boys, anyhow?'

'It's Rob McKee and Alf Lassiter.'

McClure stayed silent a moment before muttering, 'That don't mean a thing. You must've heard of me, though?'

'Yeah,' gave back McKee. 'I heard of a kidnapping crazy man who always killed those he took. I'd reckon Terry got lucky.'

McClure chuckled. 'He's been lucky right enough. Now, how do we get this done? We've got to kill Valance this night and get to the Brand O to collect our pay.'

McKee nodded. 'Killing this quick-draw,' he growled, 'how do we do it?'

Sherman, his mind racing and desperate to survive at any cost, blurted out, 'Valance is in Arrow Town. He's lodged at the Deep Gulch Hotel.'

'We'll hold rein a few hours,' spat McKee then. 'We'll go after him when all's asleep. We can kill and be gone before anyone knows. Afterwards we set to the Brand O and you'll give us the money.'

'Yeah,' said Sherman sombrely, 'sure thing.' He gripped Terry again and said, 'You're in too, boy? I mean, you've got to be.'

Terry felt sick to his heart but he gasped, 'Sure, Pa, I'll help you kill Reno Valance.'

16

Reno, slouched over the counter in the Deep Gulch, took his time over a whiskey. He finally glanced at the tallboy clock and got a surprise. It said 2 a.m. A mixture of his own deep musing and a jovial ambience had sped the hours.

Right now, Naylor and those other former Brand O men — flushed with money due to the up-front pay they'd received — were determined to make the most of it. In a fug of smoke and noise, cards games operated at several tables whilst others bunched along the bar drinking rapaciously.

Stan, during a break from serving, grinned at Reno. 'I got to say, it's proper business tonight.'

Reno nodded. 'This could be the start of the good times. Still, there's been some blood spilled on the way.'

Stan's look turned grim. 'You'll need to let Marshal Goodrich in Dumbarton know. He'll get word to the governor; Sherman's lands will be taken over then.'

Reno frowned. 'This Goodrich, what's he like?'

'Next to useless,' said Stan. 'It's said he's in the pay of cattle men to the south. Polk didn't trust him, leastways.'

Reno swallowed the last dregs of his whiskey and shrugged. 'I'm set for bed. I want to ride out early in the morning.'

Stan shaped his lips to answer but the appearance of his wife stilled his words. Mary Gorman, casting a curious glance at the swelled clientele at that late hour, gave Reno a brief smile.

'You'll definitely be leaving us tomorrow then?'

'Yes, ma'am. I can't see what else I can do around here.'

Mary nodded. 'We've had such tragedy these few days, we all need to take stock.'

Stan put a reassuring arm around his

176

wife. 'It's over, Mary. The bad days are finished.' He fixed Reno with a determined look. 'Reno, you'll always be welcome here.'

Reno moved towards the hotel stairs. 'Goodnight to you both.'

When Reno disappeared, Mary chided her spouse.

'Get these drunken no-goods finished and out,' she snapped. 'I'm set to bed and you best join me before too long.'

'Yes, dear,' intoned Stan throwing a towel over the beer pump. 'You're the boss.'

★ ★ ★

Terry led them in by way of a derelict smallholding to the north-east of town. At the farm's ruin, they settled their mounts in a barn and then set out on foot. Now, in an alleyway sided by unlit buildings, a murmur of noise reached them.

'Damn,' spat Lassiter, 'there's folk enough still awake.'

'Stop squawking,' growled back McKee. 'It'll be the saloons turning out. I'd reckon they'll be quiet before long.'

'Whiskey,' snarled McClure then. 'I'd kill your mothers for a drain of redeye.'

'We'll get this done with you,' said McKee icily at that. 'But listen, McClure, you stay out of our way. I got to say it: you're a sick son of a bitch.'

McClure chuckled. 'Now, boys, that's right unfriendly. We'll be rich partners; I'd say that's a good thing.'

'McClure,' growled Lassiter then. 'You always ride alone?'

In the darkness, they heard McClure sigh. A moment later, the Missouri man said sombrely, 'I've ridden so twenty years. I've owned nothing. I've just gotten by. After this is finished I'm set to Mexico where I retire.'

'Terry and me,' said Sherman sombrely, 'we'll be broke. I'll sell the Brand at a loss. I've cattle dying as we speak.'

'You'll be ruined but you'll be alive,' spat McClure.

'You'll start your life again free of

suspicion. Me, I'll be rich but hunted. Men like Valance won't ever give up seeking me.'

Terry stayed quiet. He ran fanciful plans in his mind but he knew it was a fool's thoughts. He possessed no gun. What could he do against killers like McClure, McKee and Lassiter? He didn't want Valance to perish, though. That man had helped him. As for Sherman, well his step-pa should swing but Terry didn't want that either. Despair swamped through him. If he and Sherman emerged unscathed from this, what would the future hold?

Thirty minutes later — the murmur of noise from the centre of town having quelled — McKee led the way forward. With each step along that pitch-black alleyway, Terry willed the end to this living nightmare. He thought of Stan and Mary Gorman — that amiable and accommodating couple caught up in this maelstrom of death; he prayed Reno Valance would be alert enough to defend himself. Finally, as they reached the alleyway's intersection with Arrow Town's Main Street, he thought of his recently deceased mother. He held back the sobs but he couldn't stem the tears. They blighted his eyes, running like an unstoppable torrent.

* * *

'Daniel, my son,' said Reno gruffly as he knelt by the bed. 'I'm not having you follow any trade with a gun. No, boy, you'll be educated to the best and I know your ma will see to that.'

Never good with praying, Reno inched to his feet and began to undress. Soon, snuffing out a kerosene lamp, he slid between the sheets. He lay there a while, listening as Naylor and the rest of the ex-Brand O moved drunkenly to their respective rooms. Finally, when that had quieted, he nestled his head against the pillow and pondered on home. It would be a mixed reunion with his wife and son: joy at their being together again but Leyton's tragic death muting their celebrations.

Reno closed his eyes but the audible exchange between Stan and Mary in the corridor kept him from sleep.

'Stanley. I've been in bed this past hour waiting for you.'

'I can't turn down trade. We've made profit tonight.'

'Shush and get a shift on.'

'OK, dear. We've sure got to keep in touch with Valance.'

'We will, Stanley. You know what, it makes me kind of proud to have a famed gunslinger like him in our house.'

'You always cussed quick-draws,' hissed Stan. 'You said they were money hunting sons of — '

'Shut up,' snapped back Mary. 'Enough.'

A moment later, a door thudded closed and Reno grinned. He gave a long sigh before sleep swamped the world.

17

Right now, clouds scudding across the night sky and blotting the moon, an impenetrable darkness had settled on to Main Street. It didn't matter to the assassins, though. The time they'd spent riding over those coal-black plains had adjusted their eyes to the lightless canvas of these pre-dawn hours. They gathered in the dirt road, scanning the buildings that stood aside the thoroughfare. No suggestion of lamps showed; all structures in still and silent repose.

'All are sleeping,' hissed McClure. 'We flush Valance out.'

'Yeah,' hissed McKee, 'but how?'

McClure reached out an arm and lifted a lamp off a nail in a boardwalk post. 'It's kerosene enough to make a good burn.'

Lassiter and McKee stepped quietly up to one of the boardwalks where they began to gather more lamps.

'What about me and Terry?' Sherman groaned. 'If this goes wrong and shots get fired we're unarmed.'

'If any shoot,' growled McClure, 'they'll think twice if you're in the way.' He spat at the dirt. 'Hell, you'll both take a slug for me; you're not behind me with guns.'

'Son of a bitch,' Sherman raged, abandoning any pretence to quiet. 'It'll be you — ' the ranch boss's words choked off as a noise grated along the street. A moment later, to a chorus of its rusted hinges, the double-doors of the horse barn swung open.

McKee mused on the blurred figure now standing outside the livery. He set a finger to the trigger but then waited.

'Who's down there?' the voice of Ben Moses sounded. 'You've skit my horses. I'm busy tonight and these beasts sniffed you.'

'I'll show you who!' growled McClure. A moment later, his slaying knife to hand, he moved to approach the livery.

Terry beat him to it. Overcoming his terror, the kid plunged down the street at a headlong pace.

He had to warn his friend Ben Moses of the nearness of death and he'd risk his own skin to do it. He tore across the distance, the noise of his footfalls setting back as a pounding echo.

'Ben,' he screamed as sprinted onward. 'Get inside.'

'Terry?' Ben's voice shook. 'It can't be you, boy?'

Terry hurtled on. He'd traversed most of the distance and the livery was close. Bile rose in his throat as he ran — an expectation of death with each sprinted stride. Any second, Terry felt sure, McClure's gun would bellow out. An instant later, if the scar-faced brute aimed true, death's burning certainty would strike Terry's back. He'd die there in that street, a gaping hole in his spine.

Terry quickened his speed and drove his aching body onward. No Colt's roar sounded and he reached the flung-open doors of the barn. Flooded with elation the kid swerved sharply and dived into the livery entrance, making Ben step aside.

'Hell, boy,' Ben gasped. 'What — '

His words ended with an explosive oath. Terry threw his body into the liveryman and they both crashed down on to the barn floor. A moment later, Terry lay gasping for breath whilst Ben, sitting up with a groan, rubbed a hand to his head.

'Goddamn it, Terry,' he barked. 'Why'd you belt me so?'

Terry answered with a fast lurch. He got to his feet quickly, hurtling to the doors and dragging them closed. A second later, he drove the locking beam into place with a relieved grunt.

Ben, rising gingerly, looked perplexed. 'You're supposed to be in New Mexico.'

Terry staggered across the barn and slumped down on to a hay bale. He sat there, head hung forward, his breath still coming at a rasping pace. At length, strength enough returned to talk, he gasped, 'That madman McClure held me hostage in the Green Coat Hills.'

'No!' Ben muttered. 'Don't tell me, at old Leyton's place?'

'Yeah,' returned Terry sourly. 'McClure's a crazy son of a bitch murderer. He killed Wilkes and Solomon.'

Ben's face portrayed his utter dismay. 'How many more are to die?' He moved towards Terry and laid a reassuring hand on the kid's shoulder. 'You've got free and you're safe now. It'll take them some time if they try to break through them doors.'

Terry dragged himself to his feet again. 'I need a weapon.'

'Are you crazy?' Ben wailed. 'You got away and you mean to go back out there?' Ben gulped. 'Who's on the street, anyhow?'

'McClure and two named McKee and Lassiter,' spat Terry searching in the stalls. 'Oh, my pa's out there too.' He fixed Ben with a despairing look. 'What weapons are in here tonight?'

'I've got fifteen horses stabled,' opined Ben. 'There's a rifle in each saddle.'

Terry acted quickly. He moved from stall to stall, pushing the horses aside as he checked the slung-up tack. Four stalls in, he gave a shout of triumph as he found what he needed. In one of the saddlebags, he located a Colt .45 together with a muslin bag containing nine slugs.

'Now I can do something,' he spat as he fed bullets into the chamber. 'Somebody can be on Mr Valance's side.'

*   *   *

Reno stirred and then, half awake, he tried to settle back on the pillow. A moment later, he sat upright in bed and wondered what had woken him. He listened but no sounds came. Though he ached for sleep, a sudden yearning in his lungs for tobacco made him exit the sheets. He found his pants and extracted makings from a pocket. He took some matches and ignited a kerosene lamp, and then, perched on the edge of the bed, he built a cigarette. Finally, he crossed over to the front sash window and dragged it up. A blast of cool air hit him and he shivered. He parted the curtains slightly, intending to flick his ash out to land on the board-walk awning below. He struck a match and the head burst into flame. It danced its orange glow and Reno inched the cigarette to his lips. He brought the match towards the smoke as an explosive surge of light from the street below heralded a deafening bellow and the glass of the window shattered into countless pieces.

Reno fell like a stone, slamming on to his stomach as the dispatched slug smacked into a wall with a sickening thud. Reno watched the felled match sizzle and any thought of tobacco was gone. In no time, he'd scrambled across the floor and lunged for his gun. Now, with his Remington to hand, he set to the window.

More noise stilled him — a wealth of glass shattering in the street. When that noise died, Reno inched on across the floor. He halted once more, though, and this time his guts turned. An unmistakable odour drifted into the room on the night breeze. Something burned.

'Mr Valance,' a voiced bellowed then and someone hammered on the door. 'You hear me, Mr Valance? For God's sake!'

Keeping low, Reno scurried in the opposite direction and soon dragged the door open. Outside, in the corridor, a pale-faced Stan had a lamp to hand and by its thrown light Reno looked at the clearly worried ex-Brand O men and a tight-lipped Mary.

'Someone took a shot at me through the window,' Reno advised curtly. 'It seems we've got a fire downstairs.'

'We'll be trapped,' groaned Stan. 'If that smoke — '

'We'll check the stairs,' cut in Naylor tautly. 'Until then we just won't know.'

189

'Goddamn it,' spat McClure, 'I reckon I missed.'

Valance's appearance had been like a visitation from Heaven — that backlight of a lamp, and more so the swelled flame of a struck match that allowed McClure to level his Colt to a target. It had been a once in a lifetime chance but still, to McClure's chagrin, it seemed the famed quick-draw had escaped unscathed.

'He's blessed,' McClure ranted on now without a worry of anybody overhearing his words. 'How does he do it?'

McKee studied the writhing flames now lapping through the smashed out windows of the Deep Gulch saloon.

'They'll burn for sure,' he growled.

McClure nodded before barking out, 'McKee, you and Lassiter get in the alleys. Work your way behind the hotel. I'll stay out here. We'll have the place covered then.'

A moment later, the two Nebraska

men darted across the street and were soon out of view.

'When this is done I'll put your boy in hell,' McClure snarled at Sherman. 'He thinks he's got away but I'll teach him.'

'Forget the kid,' screamed back Sherman, 'only Valance dying means anything now.' He shook his head.

'Think of the dollars, McClure, not some fool boy.'

McClure emitted a deep grunt. 'OK,' he growled, 'we'll get to killing Valance.'

Sherman shrugged. 'Like McKee said, it'll be a miracle if any survive that fire.'

Vicious Bill chuckled. 'If they do they'll die anyway. I'll shoot any I see; that way I'll be sure Valance is sent to hell!'

18

Terry moved to raise the locking beam but Ben snatched at his arm. The liveryman's grip — like an iron vice — stilled the kid.

'You're crazy, boy,' snarled Ben. 'You step out there you'll be dead like all them others.'

Terry shook his head. 'But, Ben, what about Mr Valance?'

'He chose his way,' said Ben icily. 'He's lived his life like that. Where Valance steps it's just blood and money; for men like him that's the way it is.'

'So you'll stop me going?'

Ben shrugged. 'You're a man — if you want to die so young, well . . . help yourself.'

'And you,' cried Terry. 'You'd stand by and let it happen?'

Ben moved away. He crossed to the chest from which he removed his Civil War Revolver.

'They drafted me to Georgia,' the liveryman said. 'It was hell.' He had a look in his eyes Terry had never seen before.

'Tell me, Ben.'

'I moved forward aside a drummer boy not much older than you.' Ben looked bereft. 'He pounded on that drum like he thought it would scare those Southern boys away. Soon, what with cannon and guns you couldn't hear yourself think. Well, I turned round and the kid weren't there. I saw him then. Well — I saw what was left of him.'

Terry sighed, but then he lifted the locking beam with a determined look in his eyes. 'I've got to do something, Ben. I might be young but I've got to try and help.'

'Yeah,' the liveryman intoned back. 'That's just what the drummer boy said.'

★ ★ ★

They huddled at the top of the saloon stairs, watching in disbelief as the long bar succumbed to raging flames. That fire, fed by the kerosene and driven by the breeze gusting in through the broken windows, they could not stop now.

The speed of the blaze was horrific — flames surging across the room and engulfing everything. Soon, timbers combusting with sickening noise and acrid, black smoke choking the air, they hurried into the corridor again.

Naylor slammed the hall door shut and then darted into the nearest bedroom. He returned in an instant with a sheet to hand. He plugged the gap at the bottom of the door before fixing Stan and Mary Gorman with a piercing look.

'That fire will spread up here,' he said hoarsely. 'What about the yard stairs?'

'Yard stairs?' Stan gasped. 'We never got round — '

'*You* never got round to it,' barked

Mary angrily. 'I said to put fire steps up but you wouldn't do it. We'll all fry for your tight-fisted ways.'

'There's no point in arguing,' growled Reno. 'We've got to work out how to escape.'

'What about the windows?' Naylor suggested. 'We climb out one of these bedrooms and work our way down.'

Reno nodded. 'Going out the front's not an option; whoever set to slay me will blast the first person who tries it.'

Stan threw up his arms and gave a howl of anguish. 'Hell, no — at least at the front you've got the boardwalk awnings to break your fall. At the back, there's just a straight drop of forty feet or more.'

They all stood in silence a while, each pondering the dire state of events.

Naylor broke the foreboding intro-spection.

'Sheets,' he gasped. 'We tie them together to make a rope.'

Quickly now, with this suggestion of salvation spurring them on, Stan, Mary and all the ex-Brand O men charged through the bedrooms gathering up linen. In no time, with sheets tied into chains, they selected a room in the middle of the hotel.

'I've got straw under cover down there,' intoned Stan. 'It's not much but it's better than hard dirt if someone should slip.' He fixed Reno with an imploring stare. 'I say women first.'

Reno shook his head. 'That's right gentlemanly if a ship's sinking,' he growled. 'But not much account if someone's down there with a cocked gun.'

Stan gulped and clutched at Mary. 'You'll go last, dear.'

Mary shrugged him off. 'Darn fool,' she spat. 'They've burned my home and my business to the ground; give me a Colt and I'll let them know what I think of that.'

Reno suppressed a smirk, though the situation worsened by the second. Retching smoke was seeping under the hallway door making them all cough.

'We'll go down in pairs,' Reno proffered. He jabbed a finger at Naylor. 'You set down with me. You best have your gun in your hand and primed.'

Naylor nodded. 'OK, Valance.'

Before long, all of them squeezed into that one bedroom, Reno dragged up the sash window. Feeding the sheet chains out, men anchored them whilst Reno and Naylor began to descend. A few feet down, the quickening wind took effect. Soon, buffeting gusts whipped at their clothes and made the escape treacherous. Reno cursed and struggled to maintain both hands on the rope whilst keeping the Remington in his grip. A few times the sheet rope twisted and Reno's body turned. He fought against it, determined to be face-on to any possible danger.

'Jeez,' gasped Naylor after a while. 'I almost let go then.'

'Get your back to the wall,' growled Reno glancing across and seeing the ex-Brand O man with his head touching the clapboard. 'If you take a slug in your spine you'll be down there for sure.'

Naylor gulped and worked his body round. 'It's dark as hell,' he said with taut words. 'I couldn't — '

'You see the muzzle's flame then you'll know it's a slug on the way,' Reno said sourly. 'Night lets you see death coming!'

* * *

Anna May dragged herself out of bed and lifted the mewling baby from his cot. Minutes later, the child resting belly-first over her shoulder and gurgling happily now, she shook her head.

'I don't know where they are,' she grumbled softly. 'Your pa and your great uncle should have been here by now.' She shook her head and brought her calmed child into her arms. 'Maybe he stopped a night or two in Arrow Town before setting home.' She kissed baby Daniel Reno Valance on the forehead and laid him gently on his bedding. 'If he's been drinking and such like I'll have a word in his ear.'

The baby, wide-eyed and with that blinding sparkle in his eyes, soon fell into a deep sleep.

Anna May inched to the bed and slid between the sheets. She patted the pillow where Reno's head would normally be.

'Hurry it up, Mr Valance,' she said as she closed her eyes. 'Life's just so much more exciting when you're around.'

* * *

They waited, hands hovering above their guns, tracking the shouts now echoing along the alley. Soon, voices neared and swaying light displaced the shadows. When two men showed, one brandishing a lamp, McKee gripped the butt of his Colt but he didn't draw. These locals were old — both clad in night-robes and their seasoned faces haggard more by tiredness and fear.

'What's happening?' The one with

the lantern lifted it higher. 'That gun blast just now — what the hell's burning?'

'It's the hotel,' gave back McKee, his voice layered with false concern. 'Jeez — I heard folk is trapped.'

'Dear God,' spluttered the man with the lamp, 'we best get over there.' At that, they passed by at a sedate jog, the lamp's light running up walls as they progressed into the distance.

Soon, with the alley's darkness returning, McKee spat angrily.

'Jeez,' he growled. 'The whole god-damn town's awake and setting this way. How'd we slay a man with that many eyes about?'

Lassiter sighed, jabbing a hand at the verdant glow now topping the town's roofs. A moment later, the fire itself was visible, towering, writhing flames under a monstrous colossus of smoke that combined to cast night out of the sky.

'Hell,' Lassiter intoned. 'They'll be cooked to ashes.'

'Yeah,' McKee spat. 'Valance won't

get out of that.' He hauled up his gun.

Lassiter groaned. 'Rob,' he spluttered, 'What if McClure — '

'Forget it,' barked McKee. 'That quick-draw's dead in the fire.' He loosed two slugs skyward, his gun blasts bellowing loud. 'That'll be the killing shots.' He smirked. 'We'll tell McClure we ended Valance and we'll set to the Brand O for those dollars.'

Grim-faced, Lassiter gasped, 'Then we split from McClure?'

'No way,' said McKee. 'That scar-face won't make it to the ranch.' He gestured with his Colt. 'He'll die on the way.'

Lassiter swallowed a curse and they were both soon running. They plunged down the alley as an answering crack of gunfire broke over Main Street.

Neither of them broke pace or uttered a word. They both knew, though, that if McClure had just shot Sherman Lomax this murderous enterprise would have been for nothing.

★　★　★

McClure's Colt bucked in his grip. As the gun's muzzle roared, the slug he'd sent whipped the distance and slammed into the hardware's front wall. The shot's effect was instant — the two people inching along the boardwalk darting behind a barrel.

'Stop shooting,' an anguished voice sounded. 'We've set here to help with that fire.'

'No help,' raged McClure. 'That place has got to burn.'

'Are you crazy?' a man cried. A moment later he called urgently, 'Those guns being loosed in the alleys — you minded what that's about?'

'Yeah,' roared McClure, 'it's some fellers I know; with any luck Reno Valance will be in hell.'

'Mr Valance?' the man exclaimed. 'Why you can't — '

'You sons of bitches show on this street,' growled McClure, 'you'll die like that quick-draw.'

Sherman, his mind in turmoil, sought escape. He lurched down the street in

202

the direction of the livery but jerked to standstill as one of McClure's massive hands grabbed hold of his jacket.

'This is madness,' Sherman howled, struggling to dislodge the Missouri man's grip. 'It's mass murder. Who knows how many were in that hotel but they'll all be dead.'

McClure cursed before setting to the boardwalk and dragging Sherman with him. Outside the jail, they watched mesmerized as that conflagration of flames devoured the hotel's upper floors.

McClure lifted his hat brim with the muzzle of his gun.

'None could survive that fire,' he snarled, 'but I won't rest a second more till I'm sure Valance is dead.'

* * *

The exodus down the sheet chains speeded up. Finally, with only Mary and a man called Nate Carver left in the bedroom, they made a rapid decision.

They dragged the metal-framed bed

under the window and tied the sheet's end to one of the legs. With several yanked-tight knots made, Carver beckoned Mary to go.

'You set down first. That way only I need trust to luck.'

Mary nodded and soon began to descend. Nate waited anxiously, his guts turning as smoke filled the room. A second later, unable to breathe, he hurled himself out of the window and grabbed the sheet chain as he dropped.

Below, Mary screamed frantically as Carver's weight set the sheet chain in motion.

'Oh, God, she wailed. 'I can't — '

She lost her grip, her fingers slipping and her mind strangely numbed as she plunged to earth. She shaped her lips to wail but no sound came. She closed her eyes, knowing death was near. She set to pray but then gasped as she felt arms gather her out of the air.

'You're damn lucky,' growled Reno as he eased Mary on to her feet. 'I was stood in the right place.'

Mary sighed. 'Why, Mr Valance, you've saved my life.'

'You're welcome for sure, ma'am,' gave back Reno. 'Now, I aim to end a few.'

★   ★   ★

It took time but finally they worked a couple of planks loose in the livery's rear wall. They prised them up, grunting with the effort, until the planks snapped with a deafening crack. A moment later, night air pushing through the gap, they scrambled out.

In the alley now, they both stood silent and stunned at the halo of burning over the rooftops of Arrow Town.

'I just can't believe it' Ben groaned after a while. 'I don't reckon anything can last through that!'

'Come on, Ben,' Terry cried, 'we've got to get to the hotel.'

Ben shook his head. 'But which way do we go? If we set on to Main Street, we'll face McClure. You heard them gun blasts, boy. One old liveryman and a hothead kid can't take on such as them.'

'It might be Valance shooting,' said Terry as he ran. 'Maybe some got out. They just might have done, Ben.'

The liveryman sighed before he tore after the already running kid. Madness, he mused, as he sprinted along the alleyway. Nothing could survive that blaze. To be out here, now, with such killers at large was a recipe for their own deaths. He clutched his Civil War Revolver and prayed as he ran.

19

'Wait, boy,' Ben gasped. He'd slowed to a walk, his limbs hurting with the effort of running. Thankfully, a distance ahead, Terry had halted.

'Come on,' the kid's voice implored. 'We've just got to — '

Terry's words broke off as he tracked a clatter of footfalls moving fast through the alley. A moment later, he lifted his Colt as McKee and Lassiter hurtled into view.

The two men stopped abruptly, both fixing Terry with withering glares.

'You're a damn fool, kid,' snarled McKee. 'You escape and then you jump right back into the snake pit.'

Terry's anger held sway now. 'You bastards,' he roared. 'You think I'd just stand by and let you slay Mr Valance?'

Lassiter shrugged. 'By the noise of that gun blast on Main Street, I'd say that quick-draw's dead already.'

Terry's face broke and he emitted a deep howl. 'Then I'll make you pay!' He slammed his finger to the trigger and a slug erupted from his gun through smoke and flame.

The shot missed — whistling inches past McKee's ear and sending that man to ground. As he hit dirt, McKee rolled deftly and came up fast on one knee. He drew his own gun then, loosing a bullet that tore past the kid's body and slammed into a wall.

It had an instant effect. Terry turned about and plunged out of sight.

'Come on, Alf,' bellowed McKee getting to his feet and beginning to run, 'get after that boy.'

Soon, in that alleyway, a deadly pursuit ensued. Terry and Ben Moses sprinted for their lives. Behind them, gaining with every step, McKee and Lassiter had murder in mind.

★   ★   ★

Dragging open the gate, Reno scanned down the alley that backed the hotel. That passageway — hemmed between high clapboard walls — was empty. Yet, worrying sounds resounded everywhere. Screams and shouts came. Gun blasts roared out then, echoing back down the alley from a distance away. When they'd died, the crackling intensity of the fire on Main Street took over.

'Whoever's shooting,' growled Naylor stepping close to Reno and jabbing a hand left, 'it's a few hundred yards that way.'

Reno's curt nod underscored his feeling of simmering rage. That bullet through his window; this inferno now promising to topple the Deep Gulch to smouldering dust were part of the same lethal plan. People had set to Arrow Town to slay Reno Valance. Whoever they were — and Reno could guess the names — were more than happy to see innocents slain to achieve that end.

'Say, mister,' a voice beckoned out of the shadows then.

Reno swung his gaze right and was ready with the Remington. But he watched, relieved, as an old man carrying a lamp approached along the alley at a faltering jog. When he reached the service yard gate, the oldster shook his head.

'I reckon,' he wheezed, 'that hotel will fall anytime.' He shrugged. 'When it does, you don't want to be near.'

Reno nodded. 'Can you get these people safe?'

The man nodded. 'My place is a distance off. The fire won't get it and nor will those loosing off their guns.'

Reno nodded. 'I thank you, friend. Show them the way.'

Naylor grabbed at Reno's arm. 'Are you mad? You can't — '

'They're here to kill me,' Reno returned firmly. 'They'll get the chance but it'll be face-to-face and not out of the shadows.'

In no time, the procession of escapees from the blaze filing along the alley led by the old man, Reno spun the chamber of the Remington and prepared for the show-down.

Stan hesitated before leaving. 'Who is it, Valance?'

'McClure's there,' said Reno icily, 'Wilkes and Solomon as well. Maybe that pair who grabbed Sherman at the Brand O too.'

'You can't take five men on, Reno,' said Stan balefully. 'You reckon that even you can do that?'

Reno didn't answer. He stepped away and Stan watched as the quick-draw stalked out of sight.

'Shoot fast and true, Mr Valance,' Stan intoned as Reno moved out of sight, 'for the sake of us all.'

* * *

McClure — confused and aggravated by the lingering gunfire — gave a growl. He'd dragged Sherman Lomax further along the boardwalk, halting where he adjudged they'd be safe should the hotel collapse. This it did now — its

211

frame buckling under the raging heat and the entire fire-ravaged mass crumbling to its foundations in a diabolical implosion of flames, smoke and sparks.

'That's done it,' the Missouri miscreant spat as the felled structure settled in a smouldering remnant of rubble. 'If the quick-draw didn't get out of that, he's in hell sure enough.'

'That gunfire,' gulped Sherman. 'Some of them folk must've got out. Why would McKee and Lassiter — '

'They've done what I asked,' cut in McClure. 'Now they've got to die as well.'

Sherman, feeling desperate but appalled, shook his head. 'Won't you ever stop? How many folk can one man kill?'

McClure grinned. An instant later, he dragged Sherman across the street and made for the alleyway that McKee and Lassiter had progressed along earlier. He blasted his gun as he moved, sending the two men who still squatted in the shadows scrambling away. In no time, that first alleyway traversed, they emerged into the passageway that ran adjacent to the back of Main Street.

'Left to the livery,' McClure muttered as though setting himself directions. 'Go right, we move up behind that burned hotel.' He pinned Sherman with a questioning look.

The ranch boss shrugged before growling, 'As you say.'

A sudden explosion of gun roars from the direction of the livery stayed McClure's reply. He levelled his Colt.

'Damn it,' he spat angrily then, 'what they doing down there?' He shook his head before growling out his own answer. 'I'd say they've set after your boy.'

Terror flooded through Sherman. They'd slain Valance and now sought to end Terry's life for escaping their clutches. His fear and culpability were as nothing now. He lunged for McClure's gun and an instant later, felt a force strike the side of his head. Pain raged and Sherman slumped to his knees. He held there, his skull hurting and unconsciousness threatening to overtake him.

'Please,' he gasped. 'I just want my boy. I already said you can have the money. God alive, now that Valance is — '

'Valance is what?' a voice sounded from the alley's shadows.

Reno, hiding there, had heard it all.

McClure turned fast, his finger slamming at the trigger, sending a slug through a surge of smoke. As his gun's blast died, he strained his ears for any sign he'd struck his prey. A moment later, his guts lurched as a voice baited him from the dark.

'It's got to be you, Vicious Bill; I've waited a heck of years for us to set to the same site.'

McClure dragged the still stunned Sherman up and positioned the ranch boss as a shield. He prodded his Colt's muzzle to Sherman's head and roared, 'I'll slay Lomax, quick-draw. I'll kill him, Valance, you hear me?'

'Do it,' spat Reno. 'He's up to his neck in it, as I reckon.'

'Dear God,' Sherman screamed. 'I'm

innocent in this, Valance. I just wanted my boy safe. This man took him and wanted my dollars unless I did what he said.'

McClure gave a derisive laugh. 'You were right, Valance,' he barked. 'Sherman here set it up; he wanted you dead and got us three to do it for a heck of dollars.'

'Three of you?' queried Reno. 'I made it five: you, Wilkes, Solomon and that pair of scum who escaped me at the Brand O.'

'Err . . . yeah,' McClure yelled after a moment's hesitation. 'That's right, I meant five.' He pressed the muzzle of his gun against Sherman's skull and hissed, 'You say a word, I'll blast you out of this world.' An instant later, dragging Sherman with him, McClure began to retreat down the alley toward the livery.

'I hear you moving,' called out Reno. 'I need you to stay and we'll get this settled, Vicious Bill.'

'I heard you'd got nine lives,' growled McClure maintaining his firm grip on

Sherman's jacket. 'I mean, hell, I set here with enough men to kill you, and you're alive and safe in the shadows.'

'It didn't matter to you,' Reno snarled, 'that innocents might get killed in that fire? You'd slay that many to end me?'

'I do what it takes,' snarled McClure. 'If the whole goddamn world needs to die to see you buried I'll do it.'

Sherman, ignoring his terror and McClure's threat of instant death, resolved to speak.

'McKee and Lassiter are after my boy, Valance,' the ranch boss howled.

A second a later, Sherman groaned as the butt of McClure's gun again smacked against the side of his head.

Reno pondered those names. Lassiter meant nothing to him; McKee stirred something in his memory. He linked it then. He thought back to that ambush at the Brand O and the man he'd slain. Before that man had perished, he'd yelled out two names. Yes, Reno mused, he cried out to a Rob and Alf.

'I heard of a Rob McKee out of

Nebraska,' Reno shouted. 'I'm guessing that's the man?'

'You got it right,' spat back McClure. 'That's one of the sons of bitches who've let me down.'

A long silence prevailed — a tension-filled hiatus through which McClure considered his options. Finally, hauling the bloodied and stunned Sherman with him, he charged down the alleyway toward the rear of the livery. He shot behind him as he ran, willing that each sent slug somehow managed to kill his nemesis. If it didn't, McClure knew full well, his heinous life might end this night in Arrow Town.

*   *   *

McKee jerked his gaze around as that solitary gunshot blasted out. When the echo faded, he stared intently at the rear of the livery building.

He and Lassiter had gotten very close. They'd gained most of the distance on the kid and the man who ran with him — presumably the horse tender. The youngster and the liveryman had been lucky though. They'd evaded the slugs and then dived into a gap in the livery's back wall.

'Jeez, Rob,' groaned Lassiter. 'You reckon it's McClure shooting behind?'

'It's got to be,' barked McKee. 'That man's wound up so tight he'll shoot at his own shadow.' He spat at the alley's dirt.

Lassiter, unconvinced, whined, 'You don't think Valance — '

'He's cooked,' raged McKee. 'I already told you that.'

'We've got to go,' screamed Lassiter as panic began to overwhelm him. 'This has gone wrong from first to last. I'm not dying here, Rob.' He began to navigate his way to the passageway that gave access on to Main Street.

A second later, with a low curse, McKee sent two slugs slamming into the livery wall. He plunged after Lassiter then, pondering angrily if they could salvage anything out of this whole, sorry mess.

20

McClure stopped running and glanced around. He gave a low curse, musing agitatedly at the silence behind. The noise of the Main Street fire had ended, only the intense stench of the smouldering embers alerting the senses to what had occurred. Right now, expecting the echo of Valance's footfalls to be loud through the alley, McClure felt unease that he heard nothing.

The noise of Sherman Lomax's suffering sounded now. The ranch boss wheezed, gasping for air. The cattle baron, his jacket still in McClure's unescapable grip, neared exhaustion. This seemingly endless night of terror and effort had taken its toll.

'I got to rest,' spluttered Sherman. 'I'm too old for such — '

'Shut it,' McClure hissed. He listened intently again, detecting fast movements

219

from the direction of the livery. He shoved Sherman aside — the ranch boss stumbled to his knees with a pained grunt. McClure levelled his Colt and waited.

It didn't take long. An instant later, McKee and Lassiter showed, both of them silent but with their gun hands twitching.

'Good to see you again, boys,' drawled McClure. 'I just come to see if you'd done what we agreed.'

McKee shook his head. 'Valance got out the hotel but we shot him,' he muttered back. 'Yeah, he died sure enough.'

'So it's settled then?' McClure returned with a curious note to his voice. 'We'll set to the ranch for a future of dollars.'

McKee nodded. 'Yeah, I reckon we could.'

McClure raged as he pondered what to do. Facing him were two scum-dog liars; behind was the avenging Remington of Reno Valance.

'Did you kill that boy?' McClure pressed, resisting his urge to scan back to check for any advance of the quick-draw. 'He deserved that and it's no mistake.'

Sherman, aching and desperate, dragged himself upright.

'Say it isn't true; I beg you, say you didn't slay Terry?'

'No,' Lassiter returned sourly. 'The boy got away. He's holed-up in that livery and it was him doing the shooting.'

Sherman's relieved sigh was audible.

'Thank God,' he exclaimed. 'Look, fellers, we'll set to the Brand O and I'll give you the money. There isn't any point — '

'There's every point,' Reno's hard-edged words interrupted. He stepped out of the shadows, his undetected steps having brought him to his killing point.

McClure spun and fired, a slug thundering out of the miscreant's Colt in a blaze of flame. A second later, as Reno dived to ground, the bullet tore into open space.

Reno rose fast, his Remington primed but he didn't shoot. Instead, he watched with mounting fury as McClure, using Sherman as a shield again, backed away towards McKee and Lassiter.

'You loose that six-gun,' growled McClure, 'this ranch man dies; I already told you that.'

'And I already said I don't care,' Reno drawled. 'You'll all hang — Sherman as well. You're dead men and it's up to you how you go.'

'You can't take all three of us,' spat McKee levelling his own pistol. 'Hell, who d'you think you are?'

'I'm the Ace,' said Reno icily, 'and I've dealt the death card to more men that I can count.'

McClure gave a nervous chuckle. 'I reckon now, Valance, you've maybe bit off more that you can chew.'

Another voice sounded — high-pitched, layered with apprehension. Yet, it was a voice made brave.

'Not if Mr Valance has got help.'

Terry stood to their rear, the

purloined Colt he'd used earlier still in his grip and now levelled. Moments before, he'd pleaded with Ben Moses for a drink and when the reluctant liveryman had acceded and set to his office for a bottle of whiskey, Terry had dragged aside the bales they'd stacked against the livery's back wall and crawled out again into the alley.

McKee and Lassiter inched round and faced the kid.

'Terry,' called out Reno with mounting worry. 'I don't — '

'No, Valance,' spat McClure. 'I reckon the boy's showing here has worked just swell.'

'Oh, God,' wailed Sherman. 'You was safe, Terry and now you've put yourself in hell's face.'

'You need to know something, Mr Valance,' shouted Terry trying to stop his gun arm trembling. 'I'm guilty of trying to fleece my pa. I agreed with McClure there to feign a kidnapping to get Pa to pay up.' Terry shook his head. 'After that . . . well, the killing started.'

'I take it,' Reno drawled, 'you had no part of that?'

'No,' Terry answered tensely. 'I'd never kill unless it was murderers such as these and I had the word of the law to do it.' Terry gulped. 'You're the law, Mr Valance, so I'm asking.'

'Don't be goddamn stupid, boy,' Sherman screamed. 'You're not thinking straight.'

McKee and Lassiter bristled and levelled their own revolvers.

'You're a young age to be eaten by worms,' growled McKee menacingly. 'You stupid son of a — '

A thunderous bellow ended all talk. Unheard as he'd inched out of the livery, Ben Moses had his Civil War revolver to hand and sent a slug over Terry's shoulder and hurtling into Lassiter's forehead. The outlaw gave a dying grunt as the bullet tore through flesh and bone. An instant later he dropped like a rock to lie in a crumpled, lifeless heap on the dirt of the alley.

224

Carnage erupted then. McKee, getting off a shot, sent a slug that belted into Terry's right shoulder and sent the kid spinning back with a scream of pain and horror. His gun thrown out of his hand, Terry slumped to his knees where he held sobbing and expecting death.

McKee didn't stop there. A second shot brought Ben Moses down — a slug to the liveryman's guts ended that issue. Ben lay on his back, his hands clutching pathetically at the gaping wound in his stomach.

McKee lurched about to face Valance but he didn't make it. A bullet from Reno's Remington tore into the back of the outlaw's skull spraying blood and brain. McKee, his head decimated, died several seconds before his cadaver touched earth.

McClure, one arm wrapped now around Sherman's neck, began to retreat.

Reno, lowering his arm, rested the Remington muzzle down against his right leg. Finally, McClure halted. He passed the corpses of McKee and Lassiter; he'd moved beyond the weeping Terry and the grievously injured Ben Moses. Now he just stood, shielded by the held figure of Sherman Lomax at a distance he felt sure that even Valance couldn't make.

'I fouled this one,' the Missouri miscreant snarled. 'It's just . . . ' He trailed off and was silent a moment.

Reno's words came, laced with bitterness. 'It was just what?'

'I heard you'd gotten old, Valance. I heard you'd turned to the settled way. Hell's teeth, I got it wrong.'

'Yeah,' Reno growled. 'You surely did.'

A massed clicking of gun hammers sounded behind Reno and Naylor's voice bellowed out.

'We're here to back up the deputy sheriff. We didn't feel right leaving him to fight alone so I'd give up, mister.'

McClure shook his head. 'You know I can't swing, Valance,' he spat. 'That's no way for a man like me to go.'

'A man like you?' retorted Reno. 'To call you vermin would be to discredit rats. You're the scum-belly of this world.'

McClure, jabbing his gun over one of Sherman's shoulders, jabbed the muzzle toward Terry. 'I'll blast the boy.'

'No,' said Reno calmly. 'You'll let Sherman and his kid alone; then you'll face me man-to-man.'

McClure sighed. 'You know I don't read, Valance. Hell, I never did get the learning.'

'Yeah,' returned Reno less harshly then. 'I was the same once.'

'This feller in Missouri,' McClure went on. 'He read me something about you and this man Buffett.'

'Yeah,' Reno said, 'he said fame came — '

'No,' spat McClure, 'you're just not getting it.'

Reno shook his head. 'What are you trying to say?'

'I remember Buffett,' said McClure with agitated words. 'You killed him but

Buffett's name lived on in words.'

Reno understood it then. 'I killed him across ninety feet,' he said. 'What do you reckon?'

McClure threw Sherman to the dirt and gave a shrug.

'It's more than that I'd say. Hell, it's above a hundred.' He slid his Colt into its holster and grinned. 'I can't lose — I won't hang leastways. If I should kill you, Hired Ace, then I'll be famous. If I die by your gun I'll still have my name read.'

Reno sighed. 'That's about the stack of it.' He reholstered his Remington and prepared himself.

With total silence prevailing in the alley now, Terry's sobs having petered out, the minutes passed, taut with tension. Finally, with a resigned grin, McClure lunged for his gun.

Reno's last thought as he hauled up his Remington was of his son. He pictured Daniel in his cot, his smiling face and gurgling attempts at words. Who was to say, but perhaps, when

Daniel's language developed enough his first utterance might be 'Pa'?

Reno let the smoke settle from his Remington's muzzle and watched as McClure slumped to his knees. The Missouri miscreant held there a second, his rugged, death-soiled hands clutching at his own slug-pierced throat. When McClure fell — crashing on to his side — he gave out a guttural wail.

Reno stepped the distance and gazed down into McClure's wide-open but lifeless eyes. He'd eradicated from the world a despicable, worthless curse.

21

'No, sir,' the manager of the Western Union Bank in Dumbarton pronounced curtly the following day as Reno sat expectantly in the office. 'If Gifford had such money he didn't deposit it here.'

A few hours later, back in Arrow Town, Reno watched the grisly spectacle of the photographing of the outlaws' corpses. The picture taker insisted that McClure, McKee and Lassiter should be posed, lashed by ropes to timber planks, against a backdrop of open coffins.

'It's the way the newspapers like it,' the man with the photographic box remarked as Reno strolled by. 'I don't suppose — '

'Not a chance,' Reno growled. 'My gun days are over.'

Soon, seated in the law office, Reno glanced across the desk at a grim-faced Stan Gorman. The owner of the now destroyed Deep Gulch Hotel brandished a bottle of whiskey and two shot glasses.

'I lent these off Callaghan at the hardware,' Stan intoned. He put the bottle and glasses on the desk and rubbed the ache of sleeping a night in the livery from the back of his neck.

'I take it you had no luck with finding a sheriff?'

'No,' returned Reno dispensing two shots of redeye. He passed one to Stan and, taking up the other, sipped at it with a satisfied gasp.

'Tell me.'

Stan swallowed his whiskey and grinned.

'That fool boy Terry will be OK, of course. Ben, well it's looking better. He's awake and the slug's out. He's a chance.'

Reno stood up. 'I've got to — '

'You've got to go home,' Stan said with a frown. 'I know that, Reno. Tell me, though, what do we do about Sherman Lomax?'

Reno shrugged. 'If I was law here he'd hang.' Reno shrugged. 'I'm not though and it's for you people to decide.'

A rap on the door stopped Stan answering. A moment later, Sherman and a bandaged Terry showed.

'I'm glad you're all right, kid.'

'Look, Valance,' growled Sherman. 'I heard what you said and you're right, of course. I've done a heck of wrong: I beat on this boy; I got in with those outlaws and I set to have you killed. I only did it to keep my boy safe.'

Reno shrugged. 'Like I said to Stan, it's not my call.'

Sherman reached into his jacket and produced a sizeable fistful of bills. He deposited the money on the desk.

'There, Stan,' he intoned. 'It's forty thousand to be going on with. Get the Deep Gulch rebuilt, bigger and better and I'll pay what it takes.' He gave a sigh. 'Please, Valance, I'll make amends. From here to my grave all hereabouts will say Sherman Lomax was a fine and good neighbour.'

Stan lifted the pile of dollars and shrugged. He stared at Terry.

'What do you think, boy?'

'Me and Pa will start again,' returned the kid. He strode up to Reno and fixed the famed quick-draw with an admiring look. 'You'll come back to visit us, Mr Valance, occasionally?'

Reno stood, smiled and shaped to leave. 'You can count on it.' Near the door, Reno turned, slid on his Stetson and sighed. 'It'll be some time till I do see you again. I need to be with my wife and child.'

Then he departed. He climbed on to his pinto and rode the trail for five wearying, sun-scorched days.

Behind him, Arrow Town changed. True to his word, Sherman's benevolence knew no bounds. The Deep Gulch arose out of the ashes; Sherman hired on and kept contented and loyal hands. He had to take on a new chuck man, though, as Albert Foster — having vanished from the face of the earth — was never heard of again. Terry, his shoulder healed, would often visit his best friend Ben Moses who'd miraculously survived his wounds. He gave up the livery, though

— still running it but with paid help.

Months later, Reno was holding his baby when Anna May walked into the living room of their home in White Falls.

'What are you doing, Mr Valance?'

He proffered the child and grinned. 'He's got my eyes; he's got your brains, I'd reckon.'

Her grief quelled enough now, she told him. An hour later, grunting with annoyance, Reno had alerted Sheriff Fitz and had gotten his pinto saddled. As he headed out of town — west again — he glanced back.

'Under the floorboards, Mr Valance,' Anna May yelled holding baby Daniel up. 'And don't dawdle.'

'You're one pushy woman,' Reno growled as he raked spurs.

At that, he and the mare hurtled into the obscurity of dust.

His life had never really changed. Sure, he had a wife and child to return to, but ahead it was always the juxtaposition of death or friends. He went back to the latter now. Back to Arrow Town — to good company, good whiskey and a soft bed in the Deep Gulch Hotel.

He dragged out that latest paper that proclaimed his slaying of three heinous outlaws, all of them gunned down from a distance exceeding a hundred feet. All those dregs of life — the headline proclaimed — Reno Valance had dispatched to hell with a slug sent by the fastest draw the West had ever known.

Reno cast the paper aside and shook his head. He'd get that fifty thousand dollars from under Leyton Gifford's floorboards and retire. After this — well . . . no hope, want or plea — in fact nothing in this vast, unfathomable world would lure the Hired Ace to ride again!

THE END

We do hope that you have enjoyed reading this large print book.

Did you know that all of our titles are available for purchase?

We publish a wide range of high quality large print books including:
Romances, Mysteries, Classics
General Fiction
Non Fiction and Westerns

Special interest titles available in large print are:
The Little Oxford Dictionary
Music Book, Song Book
Hymn Book, Service Book

Also available from us courtesy of Oxford University Press:
Young Readers' Dictionary
(large print edition)
Young Readers' Thesaurus
(large print edition)

For further information or a free brochure, please contact us at:
Ulverscroft Large Print Books Ltd.,
The Green, Bradgate Road, Anstey,
Leicester, LE7 7FU, England.
Tel: (00 44) **0116 236 4325**
Fax: (00 44) **0116 234 0205**

Other titles in the
Linford Western Library:

GONE TO BLAZES

Jackson Davis

In the Longhorn saloon in the rambunctious gold rush town of White Oaks, New Mexico, young sawyer Vince falls for the beautiful dancer Selina. But he stands no chance against Texan killer Cotton Bulloch, who kidnaps and brutally forces himself on her. Meanwhile, Jake Blackman and his boys flood the area with forged greenbacks. Can Sheriff Pat Garrett put paid to both Bulloch and Blackman? Must Vince face the murderous Texan alone? And is his love for Selina doomed?

AGAINST ALL ODDS

Hank J. Kirby

Matt Ronan didn't even carry a gun. It wasn't necessary when he was so good with his fists. But after a fatal altercation with a kid, he began to see he was perhaps too good — especially as the boy had a mighty powerful father and brother who would be waiting for Ronan when he was finally released from prison. It seemed like the moment to start packing a gun. He was going to need every advantage he could get . . .

BLOOD TRAIL

Corba Sunman

Greg Bannock raises cattle with his father Pete, until rustlers steal their herd — marking the beginning of bad times for their family. But hiding behind a mask of respectability, there is a renegade at work . . . Assisting deputy sheriff Mack Ketchum, Greg finds himself caught up in a plot to kill the rustler gang boss and has to shoot his way out of trouble, still determined to retrieve his herd. When the gun smoke clears, there is a trail of blood throughout the county.

THE VENOM OF IRON EYES

Rory Black

The notorious gang led by Peg Leg Grimes is headed to the remote and peaceful town of Cooperville to rob the bank of its recently obtained horde of golden eagles. But unknown to the gang, the bounty hunter Iron Eyes is in town to collect a reward. When the bank explodes into matchwood, Iron Eyes vows to get the money, and the outlaws — for Grimes has made one mistake: he has stolen Iron Eyes' prized Palomino stallion to make his escape . . .

MONTAINE'S REVENGE

Dale Graham

Days before the end of the Civil War, Sergeant Cody Montaine is gunned down and left for dead by a bunch of deserters led by Butte Fresno. He survives the vicious attack, but loses his memory. Taking the name of Lucky Johnson, he sets out to piece his life back together. Periodic recollections lead Cody to the town of Las Vegas, where Fresno has assumed his identity. Will Cody get revenge and so exhume his old life?

A TOWN CALLED PERDITION

Lee Lejeune

Jesse 'Mav' Bolder heads into Pure Water, known as Perdition because of its evil reputation. There he encounters some very shady characters, among them the sheriff, Bill Bronco, and local rancher Bunce and his hired killers. But there are good people in Pure Water too and when Mav befriends them, Sheriff Bronco sees it as an opportunity to run them off, leading to a bloody showdown for control of the town.